FiNDiNG MY HAT

FINDING MY HAT

John Son

SCHOLASTIC INC.

New York Toronto London Auckland Sydney
Mexico City New Delhi Hong Kong Buenos Aires

No part of this publication may be reproduced, stored in a retrieval system, or transmitted in any form or by any means, electronic, mechanical, photocopying, recording, or otherwise, without written permission of the publisher. For information regarding permission, write to Scholastic Inc., Attention: Permissions Department, 557 Broadway, New York, NY 10012.

This book was originally published in hardcover by Orchard Books in 2003.

ISBN 0-439-43539-0

12 11 10 9 8 7 6   10 11/0

Printed in the U.S.A.   40

First Scholastic paperback printing, October 2004

In memory of Uhmmah

LOSING
MY
HAT

The sudden silence of the street we'd turned onto, *Uhmmah*'s gloved hand tightening around mine.

It's the first thing I remember — two years old, huffing along on short, stubby legs, trying to keep up with Uhmmah's heels clicking against the pavement. Empty paper cups skittered along the curb, sheets of newspaper fluttered around parking meters. Steel and concrete buildings shot up into blue sky. A gust of wind sweeping down the street left us shivering into our scarves, dust and grit needling our eyes. Suddenly my head felt lighter, and I blinked up to see my hat rising above us. "Oh!" cried Uhmmah, throwing her hand up after it, but the little brown acorn top she'd knitted was already out of reach. Our necks bent back, we watched it climb higher and higher, quickly a small dot, then gone over a distant roof. We gaped at the empty space where it had vanished, as if someone might throw it back. When no one did, I turned to Uhmmah to see what I should do. She looked down at me and raised her brows with a smile. I raised my brows, too, but my mouth stayed "Oh!"

"It's gone!" she said, her dark brown eyes as wide as the "Oh!" of my mouth, and then she shook her head and laughed until she noticed I wasn't laughing with her. She leaned down to tighten my scarf and kissed her nose to mine. "Don't worry," she said. "I'll get you another one."

And she would. I've got all these embarrassing pictures to prove it. Bright red cowboy hats, things with puffy white pom-poms on top, caps with earflaps. Early on you could see the importance headgear would play in my life.

SMELLS
IN A
DREAM

One day Uhmmah and *Ahpbah* took me to a new place, crouched down in front of me, and said in Korean, "Be a good boy, Jin-Han. We'll come back for you later."

Where were they leaving me?

"Nuh-soor-dhee school," Uhmmah said in her stumbling English, not really clearing things up for me.

It was cold there, chilly with painted concrete walls and gleaming floors squeaking underneath our shoes, though I didn't mind the occasional wave of goose bumps blushing across my skin. From a window I could see the street far below, packed with cars like marching ants and molecules of people bunching up on corners, one of them Uhmmah. In the building across from ours, men and women in suits and skirts hurried about as if they were afraid of something — dashing between desks piled high with papers and files, lunging for phones and laughing too hard at something said on the other end. Back where I was it smelled like boiled corn, peas, and nervous children.

Most of the time we were napping, or being forced to. I didn't like naps. Once I was awake I wanted to be on guard in case the wind came back.

There was a group of older boys always huddled off in a corner, their ring of backs hiding some secret activity. One of the women who took care of us usually kept an eye on them, but never bothered to investigate what they were doing. Whatever it was, I wanted to be a part of it, not sitting alone, Indian-style, stacking brightly colored plastic doughnuts over and over again. Eventually I got rid of the doughnuts and started using the stand as a hammer, banged it against the floor, my knobby knees, my head. One day I whacked myself too hard and forgot where I was, stood up and staggered over toward the circle of boys. Before I knew what I was doing, I squeezed through their shoulders.

I was surprised to find a Sears catalog with half its cover torn off. But once I got up on tiptoes I saw what all the fuss was about: page after page of brightly colored blocks and balls and bicycles and games we'd beg from our uhmmahs and ahpbahs as soon as they came to pick us up. Large green worms we could ride off into the sunset. Egg-shaped people who never fell down. Once the boy who actually turned the pages got to the end, he quickly flipped back to the beginning, almost in a panic that our dream might end. Sometimes he went too far and we'd catch a glimpse of tall, elegant women smiling in their underwear, and we'd yell at him to get back to the toys already.

The whole time, this nagging feeling below my stomach kept tugging at me, but I couldn't be bothered with figuring out what it was. Pushing it away by squeezing my legs together only made it harder to balance on my toes. And then too late to stop it was running hot and wet down the legs of my pants, into my shoes, and onto the floor. Our noses twitched at the rich, vitamin odor. But who notices smells in a dream? Toy after toy we kept turning the pages, all of us standing in a wet-warm puddle spreading.

"BOYS!"

The sudden voice, like a whip cracking, jolted us out of our dream — "What's going *on* here?" We scattered and found ourselves under the glare of Mrs. Petrie, her white hair growing whiter as her face got redder. She jabbed a fat, pink finger at the yellow glaze spreading across the floor. "Who did this?"

I kept quiet and so did the other boys, though the dark, wet continent on the front of my red corduroys gave me away. I looked up to find everyone staring at me, standing there with my lips trembling, unable to figure out if I should cry or smile. The next instant I was airborne, carried like a rag doll into the boy's bathroom, and before I knew what was happening, thrust down in front of a toilet and rudely de-pantsed. I covered myself, which made Mrs. Petrie's face redder. "Go!" she demanded, and slapped my hands away as if I already hadn't. But even as I felt my eyes brimming from the stinging in my hands, all I could think about were the boys in the other room and the toys and games devoured by their hungry eyes: Lite Brite, Barrel of Monkeys, Connect Four — anything to take me away from what I was feeling there in the bathroom, the seconds ticking slower and slower as we looked down at what Uhmmah called my *khochu* (the Korean word for hot pepper), and waited.

"Go!" Mrs. Petrie yelled again, and her shrill voice ricocheted off the scrubbed tile and gleaming porcelain into my heart. The corners of my lips sagged, my vision blurred. I tried and tried until I burst into a blubbering mess of drool, snot, and hiccupping. And just like that I could see all the anger in Mrs. Petrie's body vanish out of her. Her fists unclenched and slid off her hips. A long sigh followed. She crouched down as best she could to sleeve-wipe my dripping face, then took off my pants and cleaned and patted me dry, bustling off for a moment to get an empty Wonder bread bag for my soaked underwear.

Once I was re-pantsed, she led me into another room and laid me down onto a padded floor mat. I plummeted into sleep, yet it seemed like only moments later when I opened my eyes and found Uhmmah smiling down at me. "Wake up!" she said. "I've got a surprise for you!"

I bolted up and tried to see what it was, my mind ablaze with pages and pages of toys. I could tell she was holding something behind her, and I leaned to the side to see what it was, but she twisted away to keep it hidden. I leaned even more until I was nearly lying down again. And then she laughed and brought it out the other way, slipping it onto my head before I could see what it was. When I reached up to pull it off, Uhmmah grasped my hand and raised me onto my feet.

At the elevator, Mrs. Petrie came running up to us and handed Uhmmah the Wonder bread bag holding my wet underwear.

"What's this?" Uhmmah asked.

"Oh," Mrs. Petrie said. "Let's just say it's a surprise."

Outside, wheels the same height as me slowed down in screeching protest, and up steep steps I climbed as much as I was pulled by Uhmmah. The clickety clatter of coins finding their slots, and a long, warm bus full of strangers looked up to see who'd gotten on; the hiss and squeak of the door as it closed behind us.

"Uhmmah," I said, and began listing off the toys still bright in my head. I bumped into her leg, and then squirmed at the ticklish pressure in my armpits from being lifted into the air and onto a seat.

A wrinkly old man sitting across from us started making faces at me. He crossed his cloudy, gray eyes and puffed his cheeks out around his pinched-in lips. On top he wore a hat with earflaps and on bottom a patchy beard. When he reached up and flapped his earflaps, I hoped he would fly away. I probably would've started crying if Uhmmah, sitting next to me in her crisp, white nurse's uniform, hadn't started laughing.

I looked up at her, then back at the man with earflaps. Smiling now, he looked down at a large pad of paper balanced on his lap and opened it with one hand as he pulled a pencil out of his coat pocket with the other. He wet the tip of the pencil on his black-streaked tongue, then, after raising the pad at an angle toward him, began moving the pencil in short, scratchy strokes across the page. Every once in a while he paused and squinted further into the page, then looked over to where Uhmmah and I were sitting. I had no idea what he was doing. I looked up at Uhmmah and she smiled down at me, then over at the man, before turning her head to look out the bus's window. I followed her gaze and watched the storefronts change behind the people passing us by. Sometimes I made eye contact with a stern-looking businessman standing on the corner, or a worried girl glancing up from her watch. . . .

At some point Uhmmah placed a finger under my chin and gently aimed my head back at the old man. He'd turned the pad around and was holding it out in front of him. There was a face on the page, also framed by earflaps, and at first I thought it was his — but then tilting my head I realized it wasn't. And my whole face went, "Oh!" That was *me* wearing earflaps!

ALL KOREANS
EAT
KIMCHI

A key turned in the front door and I looked up to see Ahpbah coming in from work. He had a brown paper bag folded under his arm and his smile widened when he saw me looking at it. I was kneeling at the coffee table, hunched over a Big Chief pad of writing paper, my elbows planted in a spill of crayons. I was supposed to be practicing my ABCs.

A sizzle of garlic, green onions, and hot pepper paste — *khochujang* — filled the apartment.

"*Yoboh?* Is that you?" Uhmmah's voice called out from the kitchen.

"Who else would it be?" Ahpbah said with a wink in my direction. He took off his black fur hat, peppered with snow, and put it up on a high, distant shelf inside the front closet. "Mmm," he growled hungrily, noting how good it smelled inside the apartment. *"Nehmseh chohtah!"* He reached down and gripped the paper bag between his knees, freeing his hands so he could take off his gray wool coat and place it on a hanger. He shut the closet door and retrieved the bag, then paused with a grin when he saw me following it with my eyes. "Jin-Han!" He raised the bag up next to his face. "Do you think this is for you? Uhmmah and I must have spoiled you if you think every little thing we bring home is just for you." Then he noticed the mess sprawled out in front of me. "What's this? Are you drawing?" He came over and bent down on one knee across from me, and under a crumpled forehead examined the scribble I was working on. "Is that a tree?"

I looked down at the knot of squiggles and then back up at him. I didn't know it was supposed to be anything.

"So our son's an artist!" he said loudly.

"What?" Uhmmah called from the kitchen.

"I said our son's an artist!"

"Moh rah gooh?" Uhmmah repeated.

"Nothing!" Ahpbah yelled, the muscles in his neck suddenly tense. When he saw I'd caught him in his temper, he quickly switched back to a smile. "Okay," he said, holding the paper bag over the table and making a show of unfolding it. "Maybe this time you're right." He lifted his eyebrows as he slowly reached inside the bag and with even more slowness pulled out two flat, shiny pieces of black plastic. One was straight, about as long as my forearm, the other curved like a short, squat "U."

Just then Uhmmah poked her face out of the kitchen. "What's that?" she asked.

"It's a racetrack!" Ahpbah said, glancing back and forth between us, surprised by the confused looks on our faces. "For electric cars. They have little pins underneath that fit into these grooves. When you switch on the track, the cars go around and around." He held the pieces up end to end. "See?"

"It looks like the letter 'J,'" Uhmmah said, always looking for a chance to practice the alphabet. "Where's the rest of it?"

"I don't work on those pieces."

"Well," Uhmmah said, crossing her arms over her stomach. "What's he supposed to do with the pieces you *do* work on?"

"Yoboh." The warning in Ahpbah's voice told Uhmmah to stop pointing out things that didn't need to be pointed out. He gazed down at the pieces in his hands, now an "I" and a "U," and furrowed his brow. (I just wanted to get back to my crayons.) "He can run his cars over it like this," he suddenly said, passing his hand back and forth over the straight piece. "It's a start, at least. We'll get the rest of the track eventually."

"You should've waited until you had the whole track," said Uhmmah, who disapproved of doing anything halfway. Something boiled over in the kitchen and she disappeared. Ahpbah and I looked at each other. "Don't listen to her," he said, handing over the pieces as he got up to his feet. I turned the pieces around in my hands, and then looked up to find him nodding at me. I got up and padded over to a pile of toys, and after some digging and clattering came up with my blue Hot Wheels Dodge Charger. It wasn't the right kind of car — too low tech — but I could feel that Ahpbah wanted me to do something with the track. I came back to the coffee table and set the car down on the curved piece, nudged it with my finger, and watched it roll off the track and onto the table, then onto the floor, where it kerblammed into an invisible ball of fire.

"See!" Ahpbah said, roughing up my hair. "Who needs the whole track?" He went into the kitchen then, and soon I heard their voices rise and fall in a familiar pattern of jokes and worries and sudden "No!'s" and "Don't you understand's" and warnings to "Watch your voice, Jin-Han can hear you!" The sounds of pots and pans shifting about on the stove top drifted into the room. The apartment grew warmer, heavier, sleepier. My head drowsed forward, jerked up, drowsed backward, jerked up again. I tore off the sheet I was working on and drifted into the blankness of a new page. At some point I found myself picking up a black crayon and drawing a large, wobbly circle. I went over it several times, then took the blue Charger and followed the circle around and around, vrooming sleepily with my lips. By the time dinner was ready, my face had fallen into the center of the circle and wrinkled the page with drool. I was still trying to come fully awake when Uhmmah, like a mother bird feeding her young, chopsticked *kimchi* into my mouth.

"And just how're we going to get by?" she was asking Ahpbah.

I blinked fuzzily and realized I'd been moved from the coffee table to the kitchen table — and that the food in my mouth was quickly turning into an emergency.

"I don't know," Ahpbah said, slurping a spoonful of oxtail soup, called *khori komtang*, into his mouth. "But we can't afford to stay here in the city. Even with both of us working."

I reached over my plate for a glass of water just beyond my wriggling fingers, then flounced back into my chair and rapidly fanned my tongue. "Ahhh," I said in pain.

"What's wrong?" Uhmmah asked, looking over at me as she cut *bulgogi* into smaller pieces. "Too hot?" She picked up the glass and held it toward me.

I doused the fire.

"What kind of Korean are you?" Ahpbah asked, shaking his head with a laugh. "Can't even eat kimchi." He reached out with his silver chopsticks and picked up a dripping hunk of the spicy hot pickled cabbage, held it out in front of him, and said with a straight face, almost reverently, "All Koreans have to eat kimchi," then carefully added it to the food already bulging out his cheeks. I gaped at his shiny red face, seemingly one grain of rice away from bursting, until finally, with a gulp that involved his whole body, like a snake swallowing an egg, he worked everything down, took a deep breath, and then wiped the sweat off his brow with a napkin. "We need to open up our own business," he continued, blowing his nose loudly into the napkin. "I've been playing with the numbers, and if we save enough money . . . the Paks and the Shins . . ."

"What numbers?" Uhmmah broke in, also wiping her face, then blowing her nose. "How are we going to open our own business if we don't have any money to open a business with? And just what kind of business would we open?"

"A wig store," Ahpbah said casually, waving his chopsticks in the air.

Uhmmah's chopsticks froze in front of her mouth, a drop of kimchi sauce reddening the broth of her soup. I didn't know what a wig was.

"A *what?*" Uhmmah asked.

"A wig store," Ahpbah said, stuffing more food into his mouth. "The Paks and the Shins are moving to Mem —"

"A *wig* store?" Uhmmah said. "What do we know about running a *wig* store?"

"We'll learn," Ahpbah said. "How hard can it be?"

"How hard . . ." Uhmmah swallowed. "What makes you think I even want to learn?"

"Because," Ahpbah said, and gave her a hard look, then meaningfully pulled her gaze to where I was sitting. She stopped chewing and stared — almost through me — for a long moment. I blinked loudly back at her, then

Ahpbah, then back at Uhmmah, who suddenly looked down at her bowl of soup, shook her head, and muttered it was just her luck to have married a crazy person. "A wig store," she said almost sadly. "Who ever heard of such a thing?"

AMERICAN
AS
APPLE PIE

We moved out of the city. Nobody walked around out-side, no trains rumbled over our heads. Uhmmah told me the low, flat building across the street was where I would soon be going to school. It was covered in snow, the field around it soft and marshmallowy, an untouched white-ness, except for the lone snowman out near the goal-post, and the drunken footsteps he'd taken to get there. Overhead, the heavy, gray sky hushed everything down.

I turned away from the window and went back to ly-ing on my stomach. I tried to make everything less flat and pancaked in the drawing I was working on. The car-pet left patterns on my elbows that I liked rubbing my fingertips across while I stared at the page. Ahpbah was watching *Bonanza* on TV while reading the *Korean Journal*, a weekly newspaper written in Hangul for Koreans living in America. Uhmmah was making *junyuk* in the kitchen.

It took us a moment to realize the knocking wasn't on *Bonanza*. I looked up from my drawing, and Ahpbah looked up from the paper. The knocking continued, and Ahpbah jumped off of the couch, fumbling with his shirt buttons as he hurried over to answer the door.

On the other side stood a man nearly twice Ahpbah's size, filling up most of the door frame. "Hello!" he said loudly, a bright smile above a friendly hand thrust out in front of him. "Mr. Park?"

"Yes?"

"I'm Bill Sydlowski, your neighbor from upstairs." He pointed with his other hand.

"Oh," Ahpbah said. *"Oh!"* He leaned back on his heels with widening eyes, then suddenly remembered the hand waiting below. He grasped it and looked back up with a smile. "Hello!" he said. "Please . . . please coming in!"

"Thank you," Mr. Sydlowski said, their grins trying to outstretch each other as they eagerly pumped hands. Finally they stopped and Ahpbah stepped back into the living room. Mr. Sydlowski followed with a dip of his head. Once inside, he looked around the living room as if he were trying to memorize it. "Well, hello there," he said, finding me under the window. Then he took a deep breath and searched the air with his nose, which was as large as everything else about him. "It smells great in here. What is that?"

"Oh, yes!" Ahpbah said with a laugh. "My wife. She" — he searched for the word — "she making dinner. Please to staying! Come eating with us!"

"It certainly smells like I should," Mr. Sydlowski said. "But actually, the reason I came down was that Nancy — she's my wife — since it's snowing outside and we're all cooped up, we thought what a good time to get to know our neighbors. . . ." He gazed down at Ahpbah with an expectant smile.

"Oh?" Ahpbah said. "Yes?"

"But since you've already got your dinner on the way," Mr. Sydlowski continued, "maybe you'd like to come up later? For some dessert?"

"Dessert?"

"Yes, dessert. Dutch apple crumb pie. You'll love —"

"Pie!" Ahpbah suddenly exploded with a laugh.

"Yes!" Mr. Sydlowski nodded, smiling, but also confused by Ahpbah's outburst. "Pie . . ."

"American like apple pie!" Ahpbah went on enthusi-astically. "Dessert! Yes?"

"That's it!" Mr. Sydlowski said, and reached down to clap Ahpbah on his shoulder. "American *as* apple pie," he couldn't help adding. "That's dessert! You'll come up and try some later?"

"Oh, yes! Of course!" said Ahpbah. "We . . ." He looked back toward the kitchen and then back at Mr. Sydlowski, who stood politely in the middle of the living room, which seemed smaller with him in it. "Yes . . . ," Ahpbah continued, "wonderful . . ." But he couldn't seem to fig-ure out what to say next, until he glanced over at me and saw me watching him closely, my crayons forgotten around me. He suddenly perked up with a splashy smile and turned back to Mr. Sydlowski. "Would you liking something to drink?"

"Oh, no!" Mr. Sydlowski said, taking a step back and putting his hands out in front of him. "Thank you, though. Nancy's waiting upstairs. But you'll come up later?"

"Yes, of course!" Ahpbah said, laughing. "Dessert. We coming to you later. Thank you!"

"It'll be our pleasure," said Mr. Sydlowski. Then he glanced over at me with a winking nod. "And your son can play with our Timmy. He might be a little older, but I'm sure they'll get along fine."

Timmy, in diapers, stared up at me with a finger pulling down one side of his mouth. I didn't know what else to do except stare back at him.

Above us, our uhmmahs and ahpbahs babbled on with lots of hand gestures. Timmy's uhmmah was almost as tall as his ahpbah, but much slimmer, and her long arms moved like wands in front of her, offering Uhmmah and Ahpbah each a wedge of Dutch apple crumb pie on small, pale blue plates. She sat close to her yoboh, Bill, the two of them scrunched up against each other on the short couch. Ahpbah and Uhmmah looked even smaller than they were, sitting on the other, longer couch. While Nancy tried to explain how she'd made the pie, Uhmmah smiled seriously with the pie plate carefully balanced on her knees. She fed me a sweet, delicious forkful. Ahpbah sat forward and kept bursting into laughter. After a few drinks, everyone got so involved in laughing and trying to figure out what one another was saying, they forgot Timmy and I were there.

I stood up and decided to go exploring. Turning into

a hallway, I glanced behind me and saw Timmy follow-ing me. "Hi," I said, but his face turned red and he didn't say anything, just blinked. I shrugged and went into the hallway, poking my head into this and that room. When-ever I looked behind me Timmy was still there, standing the same distance away, blinking quietly — my own per-sonal satellite. The sound of our parents laughing grew louder and dimmer.

We ended up in the kitchen. I started going through the cupboards, looked in at cans of Campbell's soup and boxes of spaghetti and Duncan Hines cake mix — stuff we didn't have in our kitchen. Every once in a while I checked to see if Timmy was still in orbit. (He was.)

Eventually we left the kitchen and wandered back down the hallway. I stopped in front of a door I hadn't noticed before, looked back at Timmy, and then opened it. It was some sort of closet, dark and musty inside. Abandoned tennis rackets lay on the floor; a vacuum cleaner hid behind a stack of boxes. Suddenly I looked back at Timmy and waved him over with a smile. He looked behind him as if he expected to find someone there, but when he didn't, he turned back to me, and af-ter a brief pause, waddled over. Still smiling that smile I was smiling, I reached out and gently took him by the shoulders, and steered him into the closet. Once he'd stepped all the way in and turned around, we stood quietly looking into each other's eyes. In another part of the apartment one of our uhmmahs screamed with laughter.

Blink, blink.

I shut the door.

And then what started out as a low moan I wasn't even sure I heard blossomed into a wail reminding me of bad times at nursery school. It frightened me, but when I tried opening the door, I found it was locked from inside. Jerking on the door harder only seemed to make Timmy's bawling grow louder and more frantic and more terrified. Which was how *I* was beginning to feel; his voice soaring higher and higher, I cringed and thought about sticking my fingers in my ears. But before I could, I heard the thumping footsteps of our parents running through the apartment. I turned around and jumped at the sound of Mr. Sydlowski's voice booming into the hallway — "Timmy!" — followed by his surprisingly swift body, his tight-lipped yoboh, and then Ahpbah and Uhmmah.

I pointed at the closet door and burst into sobs.

"Timmy!" Mr. Sydlowski repeated, reaching the closet and yanking violently on the doorknob. The whole apartment seemed to shake, and Timmy's frantic crying grew louder. I got louder, too, when I saw the dark look Timmy's uhmmah flashed me.

Ahpbah squeezed past the Sydlowskis and herded me away from the closet. "Jin-Han!" he said, dropping to one knee in front of me, and then speaking in Korean he asked me what happened.

"*Mohllah*," I wailed, and meant it. How could I explain what happened when I didn't understand myself? I looked up at Uhmmah and she seemed to know exactly what I was feeling. With a grim face she pulled me to her side, and I buried my face into her yellow and green dress, soaking the fabric.

Timmy continued wailing inside the closet.

"Timmy!" Mr. Sydlowski yelled once more. "Turn the doorknob!" But hearing his ahpbah's voice only raised the volume of his crying.

"Do something, Bill!" Nancy said. "He's scared to death."

"I know that," Mr. Sydlowski said darkly. Suddenly he turned away from the door and hurried off down the hallway, muttering he'd be right back.

Mrs. Sydlowski stepped forward and set her hand against the door. "Timmy?"

But already his ahpbah was returning with a screwdriver clenched in his hand. Mrs. Sydlowski stepped back as he dropped down to a knee in front of the closet and told Timmy to move away from the door. Then he jammed the screwdriver next to the lock and wrenched the door open, splinters flying. Timmy tumbled out into his uhmmah's arms.

No one said anything for a few moments while Timmy and I cried against our uhmmahs. Then Ahpbah coughed into his fist as if he was about to say something, but stopped when he saw the look on Mrs. Sydlowski's face.

"Well, now," Mr. Sydlowski hurriedly said. "I'm sure this was all just an accident. . . ."

"Yes!" Ahpbah agreed. "We are so sorry. It must to have been an accident!" And he looked at me in a funny way. "Right, Jin-Han?"

I nodded, my eyes blurry with tears.

"Say to Timmy I'm sorry," Ahpbah said.

"I . . ."

"No, no, that's all right," Mr. Sydlowski said. "Nothing to be sorry about." He put his hand around his wife's shoulders. "Why don't you put Timmy to bed, honey? He's had a long day." He turned back to us. "Maybe we should call it a night? It's getting late, anyway."

"Of course," Ahpbah said, nodding soberly. "Yes, of course." And he ushered Uhmmah and me down the hallway, followed by Mr. Sydlowski. When I looked back between his legs, Timmy and his uhmmah were no longer there.

At the doorway Mr. Sydlowski shook Ahpbah's hand and tried to make a joke. "Except for the crying and door busting," he said, "we'll have to do this again sometime."

But we never did.

I saw Timmy only a few times after that, usually in the stairwell, half-hidden behind his uhmmah's skirt. Once, my uhmmah made some bulgogi and ordered Ahpbah and me to take it up to them. Mrs. Sydlowski opened the door and talked to Ahpbah while we stood in the hallway. Ahpbah kept laughing and smiling, but Mrs. Sydlowski only smiled carefully as she avoided looking down at me. Across their living room, I could see Timmy crouched in a cone of lamplight, biting into a chunk of green Play-Doh. He looked up and we exchanged blinks just as Mrs. Sydlowski, thanking us, closed the door. The next day, Mr. Sydlowski, carrying a loaf of warm banana bread, knocked on ours.

Not long after that, there were a few days when Uh-mmah and Ahpbah brought home bundles of flattened cardboard boxes, built them back up, and filled them with everything we owned that wasn't a piece of furniture. A few days later an enormous truck blocked our view of the school, and a couple of men wearing overalls came out and took the boxes and all our furniture away. After one last sweep through the empty apartment to make sure nothing was left behind, we got in our car and followed them.

Several hours later it was dark and I was too awake to sleep. I leaned over the seat and stuck my face into the alien-green glow of the dashboard. "Ahpbah?"

"Yes, Jin-Han?"

"Where are we going?"

"Memphis, Tennessee."

"Where's that?"

"Where Ehrvis Puh-ress-adee lives."

"Elvis Presley!" The only eight-track tape we had to listen to in the car was his 1973 television concert, *Aloha from Hawaii via Satellite*. I knew the words to most of the songs.

"Yes," Ahpbah said, looking over at Uhmmah, her head on a pillow against the window. Passing headlights showed her sleeping face. "The king of rock and roll," he added, then sang a few words softly: "Love me tender, love me true . . ."

And I bellowed, "All my dreams ful —"

"Shh, Jin-Han! Not so loud. Uhmmah's sleeping."

"Why?" I whispered. "Is she sick?" Ever since her stomach had grown bigger, she'd been sleeping a lot more.

"No, Jin-Han. But she needs to rest. Remember, Uhmmah is two people now. She is carrying your *dong-sehng* inside her body."

"Wouldn't it be easier to carry Dong-sehng outside? How much longer will Dong-sehng be inside Uhmmah?"

"Not much. Dong-sehng will be born in Memphis — the first person from our family born in *Mi Gook*."

"Really?" I said. "Where was I born?"

"You were born in Germany."

"Germany? Where's that?"

"In Europe."

"Where's that?"

"Across the ocean."

"Oh."

Uhmmah moaned and shifted in her seat, her hands folded over her round belly.

"Ahpbah?"

"Yes, Jin-Han?"

"What ocean?"

"Moh rah gooh?"

"What ocean?"

"Oh. The At-uh-lantic Ocean."

"Where's that?"

"Between Europe and America. Many, many years ago — so long ago — everybody coming to America that way. They taking the ship all the way across. It takes them such a long, long time. It's kind of lucky for us, because we taking the airplane. Just one day for us to coming here."

"I was in a plane?"

"Yes, that's how we coming here. Don't you remember?"

"No."

"You were so young then."

"Can we go again?"

"Of course! Someday you will go to Korea. You have to meet your family. Now be quiet. Uhmmah is sleeping."

I sat back and slid around on the long vinyl seat I was sharing with some pillows and boxes. Then I got on

31

my knees and looked out the rear window, mesmerized by the headlights of the cars behind us, watching us, weaving left and right, the red taillights suddenly passing on the other side of the highway fading into night.

"Ahpbah?" I said, my breath fogging the view. "Is Dong-sehng sleeping, too?"

"Yes, Dong-sehng is sleeping, too."

"Ahpbah?"

"Jin-Han."

"Where were you born?"

"In Korea."

"Uhmmah, too?"

"Yes. Uhmmah, too."

"Ahpbah?"

"Yes, Jin-Han."

"When are we going home?"

"We're going there now, Jin-Han."

WHAT
IT IS

It was our turn to host the weekly gathering of the Parks, the Paks, and the Shins. Sitting on colorful square cushioned mats around a low table in the middle of the living room, we darted our chopsticks toward a steaming feast of soups, stews, casseroles, and side dishes called *bahnchahn*. Underneath all the plates and bowls, completely obscured from view, were beautiful mother-of-pearl scenes of Korean village life set into the table's black lacquer.

When it was just our family eating at home, we sat at the regular sit-down table we'd ordered from Sears.

Uhmmah couldn't drink because of Dong-sehng, but it didn't stop her from joining in the frequent eruptions of laughter around the table. Ahpbah always laughed the hardest, and sometimes, getting carried away, his shiny, almost choking face made a sound like a wet rag squeaking across glass, which made everyone laugh that much harder. "Yoboh!" Uhmmah said, shaking her head down at the table. "It's not that funny." Though he didn't say anything, I saw Ahpbah's face darken as he coughed himself down to a chuckle. Then Mr. Shin muttered something out of the corner of his mouth, exploding another round of laughter. This time Uhmmah only smiled and shook her head, calmly spiraling the skin off an apple with a knife.

The Paks had two kids, James and Margaret. Margaret was my age and wore rectangular brown glasses. James, a few years older, had brought along his new magnifying glass, and bragged about all the ants he'd fried with it. Margaret, pushing her glasses up her nose, said he was gross. The Shin girls, Won-Hee and Won-Soo, said he was cruel, and had no feelings, even though their main goal in life seemed to be kicking James and me in the shins. We all had straight, shiny black or dark brown hair, the same color as our eyes.

As the night wore on, and the beer cans began struggling for space on the table, the kids were waved off into my room, which we demolished almost before the door closed. Everything Uhmmah had neatly put away beforehand was thrown into a general area of messiness, and then forgotten. Margaret, Won-Hee, and Won-Soo played with their Barbie dolls. Won-Soo's wore a white tennis outfit, but she'd lost her racket during the drive over. Won-Hee's wore bell-bottom jeans, a matching denim jacket, and rhinestone sunglasses sitting on top of her head. She'd also cut her hair short, making a fashion statement far ahead of its time. Margaret's Barbie, thanks to James, was missing an arm.

I was looking at my green Hot Wheels '57 Chevy with my chin on the floor, trying to imagine myself behind the wheel, when James, returning from the bathroom, flung open the door. "Hey!" he hissed.

We looked up to see him panting with his hand on the doorknob, as if he'd just been chased. I could see the blue and green stripes of his shirt through the fly of his brown jeans, which he'd forgotten to zip up. Won-Hee and Won-Soo snickered. Margaret pushed up her glasses and pointed. James looked down and zipped up as fast as his face went red. I got back into the Chevy and drove it to the levee. The girls continued blabbing.

"Jin-Han! C'mere!"

I looked up again to see James waving me urgently toward him. "What?" I said, not trusting people who waved me toward them.

"Just come here!"

"What is it?"

"I wanna show you something."

"What?"

"I can't say. You have to see it."

Sighing, I stood up and followed him down the hallway to Ahpbah and Uhmmah's bedroom. He opened the door and we slipped inside.

"What were you doing in here?" I asked.

He shrugged and said he thought it was the bathroom.

"Oh."

"Look." He pointed at a couple of cardboard boxes I hadn't noticed before. They were on the floor by the foot of the bed. Korean writing was scrawled on the top of each box, but I didn't know how to read it.

"What is it?"

James went over and pulled back one of the lids, stuck his hand inside, and brought out a square, clear-plastic bag with something dark and blobby inside. "Wigs!" he said, holding the bag up as if he'd won it.

"Wigs?"

"Yeah. Here." He tossed me the bag and it hit me in the face. I picked it up and opened it as he pulled more bags out of the box, then stuck my hand into a new feeling — something dry, soft, and coarse. Spongy. I pulled it out and it fluffed into a big, round black I-didn't-know-what.

"That's an Afro," James said.

"Afro?"

"Yeah, you know. Like black people." He pointed at his head. "Like Fat Albert — *Hey, Hey, Hey!*"

"Oh."

"Put it on."

"Me?"

"Yeah. Like this." He opened a bag and out fluffed an even larger Afro. He held it open in front of him and then bent forward and stuck his head into it. When he straightened up, his body looked smaller. "What it is," he said, and started strutting around like a chicken with a huge head, one leg broken.

"I thought you said it was an Afro."

"Huh?" He checked himself out in the mirror above the dresser. "It *is* an Afro, man."

"Then why'd you ask me what it is?"

He turned to me with his thumbs hooked into his

pockets, one hip pointing toward me. "What are you talking about, man? I didn't ask you what it is, I *told* you what it is. You dig?"

"Oh," I said, thinking, No, dig what?

"So put it on." He nodded at the Afro in my hand.

"Uh . . ."

"Just do it, man. It's fun."

Because I didn't want to chicken out in front of him, I shrugged and slipped it onto my head.

"Outta sight!" he said, coming up to me and adjusting the wig. He stepped back and raised his palm out toward me. "Slip me some skin, Brother."

"Right on," I said with a grin, getting into it, but missed and sort of slapped his forearm.

He snorted and shook his head. "Come over here." He threw his arm around my shoulder and pulled me in front of the mirror. "Check it out, man."

Wearing Afros, we grinned back at us. I wondered if wearing the wigs changed who we were.

"Let's go show the girls," James said, and with his arm still around my shoulder, dragged me back to my room.

When we opened the door, the girls looked up and clamped their hands over their mouths, making their eyes widen from the squeals trying to get out.

"What it is," James said, and he started strutting around like a gimpy chicken again.

"What's wrong with your leg?" Won-Soo asked.

"We're black," James said. "Can't you tell?"

"You're not black!" Margaret said with a giggle. "You're a stupid Korean."

"Shut up," James said. "Am not."

"Are too."

"Shut up both of you," Won-Hee said. "Where'd you get those from?"

"We found 'em," James shrugged.

"Yeah," I said, hooking my thumbs in my pockets. "You wanna try 'em on?"

"Shut up," James said again, slapping the back of my head. (I hated it when he did that, but the way the Afro waved around up there was kind of neat, and I forgot to complain.) He held up the three bags he'd brought with him, and was immediately pounced on by the girls. After the usual keep away and knocking over of lamps and running around like hooligans, all five of us ended up wearing Afros like it was the funniest thing in the world, our eyes squeezed shut, our mouths gasping for breath. Finally, we laughed ourselves out, and started doing things we thought people with Afros did. James continued his wounded chicken act, and Won-Hee held her Barbie doll up to her mouth like a microphone. She started singing "Fame," and then "Get Down Tonight" (neither of which were sung by black people). Eventually Won-Soo and Margaret joined in, and then when they started singing the Jackson 5's "ABC," James and I got in on the fun.

"Hey!" James broke in after about the sixth time through the song. "Let's go into the living room!"

"What!?" I was worried we weren't supposed to be wearing the wigs.

"Yeah!" Won-Hee said.

"I don't know . . ."

"Don't be a chicken," James said, rushing over to the door. "C'mon!"

"Wait!" I said, but I was already the last one in the room, and I hurried out after them.

A wordless shock, like faces surprised in a picture, exploded into laughter. "*Ominah! Ominah!*" our ahpbahs and uhmmahs shouted. "What is this? Look at these crazy kids!" And they slapped one another's knees and banged the low table as they buckled over with laughter. Ahpbah crumpled into a fit of coughing, his face about to pop. Even Uhmmah laughed so hard, she had to grab on to the arm of Mrs. Pak, who was trying to clap in time to our singing.

"What it is," James said, limping around while Won-Hee and Won-Soo did a dance-and-spin routine they must've practiced before on their own. Margaret and I tried to follow along, but we were giggling too much to do a good job of it. It didn't matter, because Won-Hee more than held us together, belting out "ABC" with all her heart, her voice filling the room.

As our parents continued laughing and clapping and clanging their chopsticks against the empty *mehkjoo* cans, Ahpbah suddenly jumped up and shouted, "What it is!" Then barely able to breath from laughing so much, he stumbled over to me and raised his hand for a high five.

"Yoboh!" Uhmmah said sharply, but no one paid her any attention, assuming she was once again keeping Ahpbah in check. But I happened to glance over and saw her looking down hard at her hands, placed on top of the table as if she were examining her nails.

"What it is!" Ahpbah said again, and laughed his high-pitched laugh, catching his breath just long enough to tell me to go get another wig for him. "Hurry," he giggled, and sent me off with a playful kick to the rear, which nearly caused him to fall backward onto the table. "Whoa!" everyone shouted, and Mr. Shin stood up just in time to catch Ahpbah and push him back into balance.

"Yoboh!" Uhmmah said louder, and I looked back at her as I turned into the hallway. James's uhmmah, Mrs. Pak, was looking closely into Uhmmah's face and resting one hand on her stomach.

Sensing something was about to happen, I rushed into my parents' room and dug out another Afro. But by the time I came back, everything had changed. Ahpbah was gone, and Mrs. Pak and Mrs. Shin were helping Uhmmah slowly cross the living room. James and Margaret and the Shin girls sat on their feet with their mouths open and silent. Only Margaret had taken her wig off, holding it in her lap as if it were the polite thing to do.

"Uhmmah?" I said.

"*Aigoo,*" she moaned. "Jin-Han, you have to be a big boy now. You're going to be an *ohpbah.* Ominah!"

Something was hurting her, and I wanted to cry. Ahpbah came back into the room, his face serious and scattered. He'd changed pants and was hurriedly putting his shoes on by the front door. He put some sandals down in front of Uhmmah and helped her slip them on. Then he took over for Mrs. Pak and led Uhmmah out of the apartment with Mrs. Shin.

"Uhmmah?" I said. "Ahpbah?"

The door shut and Mr. Shin told me not to worry, that they'd be back. They were going to get my dong-sehng.

"Oh," I said, and took off my Afro. I slumped down onto the floor and lay on my back. I spread out my arms and looked across the carpet at my hand, empty and half-curled, waiting to hold another, smaller hand inside it.

POWERFUL
RAYS

Summer dragged to a close. The grass fell in on itself, and the leaves weighed down their branches. The air was thick with honeysuckle, and hot and heavy like an extra coat you didn't want to wear. The sounds of insects going about their business grew louder and louder until I thought everything was going to burst open, but didn't, just cooled into a nightful of stars and its mysterious, invisible sounds.

One morning we drove past a group of black people waiting at a bus stop. An old woman wearing cat's-eye glasses stood perfectly still in the shade of her yellow umbrella. Next to her was a boy about my height sliding his purple tongue up and down a melting purple Popsicle, while two older kids, a boy and a girl, chased each other around a large woman who might have been their mother. On my knees at the rear window I watched her wipe her brow and neck with a handkerchief and then return it down the front of her blouse.

I turned around and slid over behind Ahpbah's seat and asked him to open his window. Warm, sweet wind blasted into my face and I opened my mouth to gulp it in — closing it when it dried out.

Ahpbah put in Elvis Presley and I started singing along. "Caught in a trap / I can't walk out / Because I love you too much, baby." I had no idea what that meant. I got up on my knees and took a quick tour of the windows to see if anyone else was on the road. I didn't see any cars and leaned excitedly over the front seat. "Go faster!" I said, and instantly had to grip the back of the seat tighter as we neared the hill coming quickly toward us, and then a burst of speed took us up the short rise until with a giddy whoop from me it felt like we'd actually left the road. "Ominah! Yoboh!" Uhmmah yipped, gripping the top of the dashboard with one hand and clutching Jin-Soo, my new dong-sehng, against her body with the other. But with a skritch, squeal, and jerk of the steering wheel, Ahpbah had us squarely down on the road again. It was like my favorite cop show on TV, *The Streets of San Francisco*, but without the siren wailing on our roof. "Faster!" I yelled, leaning far over the front seat to reach down and poke Jin-Soo in her stomach, but barely a wrinkle passed across her face — nothing like the fireworks whenever I pulled the bottle out of her mouth.

"Where are we going?" I giggled, clinging to the front seat. I always forgot to ask at the beginning of a trip.

"Kindergarten," Ahpbah said, grinning dementedly at me in the rearview mirror.

And suddenly all the fun I'd been having whooshed out of me. I flung myself into the backseat and slid over into the corner farthest away from Ahpbah, my arms crossed furiously in front of me. I glowered at the shiny green vinyl on the back of Ahpbah's seat and tried to melt through it with the feeling that I was being punished for something I didn't do. But the vinyl resisted my powerful rays.

"Again?!" I whined.

There were six of us in the class: Brian, Chet, Mary Lou, Kate, Tina, and me. Brian had brown hair and was the quietest one. Chet was always getting into trouble for chewing gum, usually because Mary Lou pointed it out to Ms. McCusker, our teacher. Kate giggled with a lot of "g's" and, except for Ms. McCusker, knew the most words. Tina had black hair that went straight down to her waist, and always smiled a little too long at me with her shiny black eyes, which made me blush, which made her laugh, and then she'd whisper behind her hand to Mary Lou and Kate, and then they'd go ha! ha! ha! about what I didn't know, which made me want to throw paste in their hair.

Ms. McCusker made seven in the class. She was tall and had straight brown hair down to her shoulders. Sometimes she wore a patterned silk scarf around her neck. She never raised her voice.

We didn't have a regular classroom in a regular school building. Ours was a trailer at the edge of an endless asphalt parking lot melting under the sun, bumper to bumper with trucks and muscle cars and beat-up hand-me-downs belonging to the high school students and teachers. We weren't allowed to jump too hard in case we fell through the floor. We were in our own little world, and Ms. McCusker was our leader.

"Class," she said to us one day. "I'm going to step outside for a little bit. But I'll be right back. I want you to sit quietly in your seats in the meantime. Will you do that?" Her gaze settled on each of us for a second. "I know you can." We grew still and silent at our desks as we watched her take her purse and step outside the door. It was the first time she was leaving us on our own.

Just before the door closed behind her, she poked her head back in and reminded Chet not to chew gum.

Twelve brows lifted, we looked around at each other, and then leaned back in our chairs to watch her through the window. With calm, even footsteps she crossed the parking lot, her body shrinking toward the large brick building on the other side, where she opened a little gray door and disappeared from view. As soon as we heard the faint squeak of the door closing behind her, and then waited another breath to see if she came back out, we forgot what she'd told us. Words gushed out of our mouths, and quickly rose into shouts, giggles, and snorting laughter, because who was there to stop us? Chet turned sideways in his seat and pulled up the right leg of his green pants, revealing a yellow sock with three horizontal green stripes. Wriggling his fingers down into the sock he dug out a stick of Bazooka bubble gum. But then before he could even finish the triumphant smile stretching across his face, Brian, the quiet one, who sat across from Chet, shot out of his seat and snatched the gum right out of Chet's hand.

Everyone froze, including Brian. And then the scrape of Chet's desk as he lunged after Brian sent the rest of us flying out of our seats, too, running and jumping and screaming like wild animals let loose. But before anyone could actually fall through the floor, everything stopped just as quickly. We'd divided ourselves into boys on one side and girls on the other. We looked across at one another like enemies on a battlefield, panting, until Chet, who'd wrestled his gum back by then, popped a big, pink bubble all over his chin. And then maybe because he was still mad about the gum, he pushed Brian into Mary Lou, which made everyone "Ooh!" in unison. Then Kate shoved Mary Lou into Brian, which made everyone laugh, including me, though maybe too hard, because suddenly Brian gave *me* a neck-snapping shove into Tina. I didn't put my arms out in time, and my lips ended up bumping into hers, which made her shriek, "Jin-Han kissed me! Jin-Han kissed me!"

"Uh-uh!" I said, jumping back away from her. I wiped my mouth just to be sure. "No I didn't!"

"Yes you did!" Kate said. "I saw it happen! Tina and Jin-Han sittin' in a tree . . ."

"Do it again!" Brian shouted, apparently a different kindergartner when Ms. McCusker wasn't around. And he pushed me toward Tina, who at the same time was shoved from behind by Mary Lou. Both of us were ready this time and we put our arms out and stopped each other, but now Brian and Chet were behind me, and Kate and Mary Lou were behind Tina.

"Kiss her again!" Mary Lou shouted, jumping up and down. "Kiss her again!"

Tina smiled at me with her dark shiny eyes, and I started to blush.

"Yeah!" Brian shouted. "Kiss her again!" And all four of them began chanting it loudly. "Kiss her again! Kiss her again! Kiss her again!" All the while Tina kept smiling at me as if there were a message embedded in her teeth. Her eyes got shinier until she calmly closed them, puckered her lips, and leaned toward me. I backed up against Brian and Chet as if I were sliding down into a pit of chomping alligators, but the little finks only pushed me forward again. "Nooo!" I cried, struggling against them. At the same time I couldn't help grinning. Not because I wanted to kiss Tina (no, never, nuh-uh), but because I kind of liked all the attention.

"See!" Kate said, pointing at my smile. "You're in love with her! You *have* to kiss her!"

"Nuh-uh!" I insisted, even though I didn't understand

what she was talking about — love? That word in Elvis's songs? I started feeling pretty desperate and came up with a desperate plan: The only way for me to get out of the situation was to out dare Tina and the rest of the class.

I shut my eyes, puckered up, and leaned forward, too.

"Do it! Do it! Do it!" the others shouted deliriously while Tina and I, peeking out of our eyes, leaned closer and closer toward each other. I closed my eyes again and teetered on the tips of my toes, waiting, hoping Tina would pull back at the very last oh-please-possible instant.

But she didn't, and neither did I, which is when gravity brought us together.

The explosion that followed seemed like miles away, as if Brian, Chet, Kate, and Mary Lou were on the other side of a glass wall, their wild cries of disbelief distant and muted. Tina, smiling as always, stood across from me and blushed, which made me blush more than I'd ever blushed in my life. I looked down hard at the floor.

And then Ms. McCusker was standing just inside the door, her open mouth mirroring each of ours. But before anything came out of hers, Kate shouted, "Jin-Han kissed Tina!" And the others forgot themselves along with her, unleashing a clamor of voices:

"Yes, they did, Ms. McCusker!"

"They're going to get married!"

"They're going to have babies!"

Until gradually, like an autumn leaf floating down, Ms. McCusker's face settled into a smile. We knew then that we weren't going to get in trouble. Except for Chet, who once again had to spit his gum out into Ms. McCusker's hand.

But rides in the car didn't always end up at kindergarten. Sometimes I went downtown with Uhmmah and Ahpbah, where the buildings were taller and closer together, like in my earliest memories of Chicago. The streets weren't as crowded or noisy, and the large, gray stones holding up the buildings were riddled with holes shaped like seashells. I liked to poke my finger inside the holes and come away with a dollop of old gray dust.

"Yah!" Uhmmah would say, slapping at my hand. "Don't touch that!"

But I already had, and would again, if not on the next block, another day. Maybe past the Walgreens where I'd gotten lost once. Ahpbah and I had gone there looking for stuff needed at the new wig store — masking tape, lightbulbs, WD-40. A song about the sun coming here rolled around the ceiling. Underneath, we snaked around the aisles and eventually turned into one practically falling over itself with toys, spilling off shelves and hooks onto the floor. Like a pirate finding treasure, I stopped and pulled down or picked up whatever I could get my hands on: Slinkys, boomerangs, yo-yos, cap guns, board games. I took each item and turned it over in my hand, fantasizing about the fun I'd have if it were actually mine.

At some point I looked up from the blister-packed G.I. Joe I was holding and realized Ahpbah was no longer there. My heart skipped a beat and then tried to catch up to itself. I started to feel dizzy. Toys bulged out at me from the shelves. I took off and quickly glanced down all the aisles, confirming what I didn't want to be true: *Ahpbah had left.* I thought about asking someone there for help, but I was worried they'd get worked up and make me feel even more panicked. Though I'd never walked anywhere on my own before, I decided the best thing for me to do was try to find my way back to our store.

My head down, I passed through the automatic doors and walked as fast as I could without running. Old men leaning on canes slowly turned their heads behind dark glasses as I hurried through the streets. Tall women, both black and white, gave me a quick glance as they sashayed along in their bell-bottoms. Men in business suits followed them with their eyes.

Finally, around the corner, past the candy store with its warm smell of roasted peanuts, I saw the sign for Lee's Wigs, named after the man we'd bought it from. Behind the windows, white posters with big red letters spelled SALE! SALE! SALE!

The bell tinkled softly as I opened the door, and Uhmmah and Ahpbah looked up from behind the counter.

"Jin-Han!" they cried.

Ahpbah rushed out toward me and knelt down in front of me, grabbing me by the shoulders. "Where did you go! You scared us to death! We thought someone had taken you! Aigoo!" He pulled me roughly to him and then pushed me away and mussed my hair. "We even called the police."

"The police?"

"Yes! They're out there now, looking for you."

I looked out the window and felt relieved that I'd made it back without running into the police. I would've been a lot more scared if I had.

Turning back, I saw Uhmmah sitting stiffly behind the counter. I was surprised she hadn't come out to hug me back. Instead she went on brushing the wig in front of her. It made my scalp hurt just watching. I could see she was furious — at first I thought with me, but then she continued snapping at Ahpbah throughout the day, and I realized she was mad at him for not watching me more closely. I felt bad because it seemed like it had mostly been my fault, but Uhmmah was in such a state I was afraid to explain it to her, and then have her get mad at me instead.

Behind her, on shelves reaching up to the tall ceiling, rows and rows of mannequin heads wearing wigs of all shapes and sizes sat silent. The same was true on the opposite wall, except instead of counters and display cases, there were three seating areas with large, round mirrors where customers tried on wigs.

The display cases were filled with combs and hair picks and cans of hairspray. One only contained small, flat plastic cases in which you could see a pair of fake eyelashes set demurely under a tube labeled EYELASH GLUE. On top of this display case was a longer-necked mannequin head wearing a proud black Afro over long, glittery eyelashes. Another display case held a variety of hairpieces, which by themselves looked like useless blobs of hair meant to be thrown into the trash until they were stuck onto the back of a woman's head, readying her for an elegant evening out on the town.

All the heads were faced at an angle toward the front of the store. It was the same face — the color of coffee and cream, glamorous, untouchable — over and over again, regardless of the style of wig it was wearing. Every time I came to the store I noticed something new about them: the long, pointy nose; the high, sharp cheekbones; the clear, dried speckles of hair spray across their plastic skin. They didn't look anything like the women who came in to try on the wigs, leaving the heads momentarily bald, yet still distant and cool, as if they knew something real people didn't.

While Uhmmah and Ahpbah helped customers try on different wigs, and occasionally sold them with a "Thank you!" and "Please come back soon!" I usually sat behind the counter, lost in a world of black-and-white TV. By my feet lay Jin-Soo in her cradle, dozing off and then waking up with a start when her bottle fell out of her mouth. (Without taking my eyes off the TV, I plugged her mouth back up before she could start crying.) But after a while the TV's pull on me got weaker, and the mannequin heads seemed to grow stronger in their presence around me. I found myself looking up every now and then to stare at one. I focused on the eyes, the nose, the lips. More and more the lips filled the screen of my eyes, and one day I started thinking about the time I'd kissed Tina by accident, and remembered the surprise and tingle I'd felt afterward. It was supposed to have been something gross and totally blech-y, but all I'd felt inside was like a beehive on a warm, sunny afternoon.

And then I thought about the times I kissed Uhmmah and Ahpbah good night, or Jin-Soo for being my dong-sehng. And how that seemed different from the Elvis concert I'd seen on TV, where the women at the edge of the stage had raised their arms and screamed at Elvis until he'd kneel down all dripping with sweat and kiss one on the lips. And the screams that came after that piercing through the music. Or how the older boys and girls in the school parking lot practically tried to swallow each other's faces, their hands clawing at their bodies, as if they were trying desperately to get away from each other.

So much seemed to happen with a kiss, and I was dying to know more. But then Jin-Soo started crying, and I looked down to see that she'd emptied her bottle.

"Uhmmah!" I cried, irritated at having my thoughts

interrupted. Her hand came over the top of the counter and reached down waiting. I handed up Jin-Soo's bottle, and Uhmmah excused herself from the customer she was helping.

"Make her stop," Ahpbah said as he now tried to help two customers.

"Shhh!" I said, leaning over the cradle, but she kept on crying, and seemed to get louder. I got off the little red plastic stool I was sitting on and knelt down by the cradle. "Jin-Soo," I said. "Don't cry. Please, stop." And I put my finger in her tiny little hand and watched her even tinier little fingers curl around it. Still, she kept crying, and I shushed and shushed but she wouldn't stop, just kept crying harder and harder. Until I leaned forward and kissed her on the nose. The waterworks immediately stopped, and she stared up at me quiet, her little feet paddling air, her teardrop eyes with their dark brown pupils blinking wetly.

PICTURE
DAY

"Wake up!" Uhmmah said, pulling back the curtains and flooding the room with light. I squinted and sat up rubbing my eyes, then sort of falling back asleep, kept my eyes closed and raised my arms. Uhmmah came over and pulled my shirt off. Usually she put another one on and I'd wear it for the rest of the day. After waiting a while I opened my eyes and hugged myself, shivering at the chill in the air. I didn't know if it was because the weather had gotten colder, or because I was alone in the room.

"Uhmmah?"

"Jin-Han! I'm in the bathroom!"

I slid off my bed and walked down the hallway. Uh-mmah was on her knees by the tub, which was filling up with water. She looked back and saw me standing at the doorway. "Come here," she said, and turned and held her wet hands out toward me. "You have to take a bath."

"Why?"

"Because," she said, and explained that today was picture day.

Oh, I thought, not really understanding. I spent the rest of the morning being washed and dressed and combed and practically shined. I was already feeling stiff wearing more clothes than I usually wore, when Uhmmah clipped a bow tie under my chin. Finally she led me over to the mirror and knelt down beside me.

"Look at my handsome boy," she said, her hands on my shoulders and her cheek against mine. She had on a light brown long-sleeved dress. Her black hair, held back with a barrette, followed her clear, pale face. Even when she smiled there was always something in her dark brown eyes that didn't.

My hair was shiny and parted down one side; whatever kept it like that must've been on my cheeks, too, the way they sparkled. I smiled back at Uhmmah in the mirror and felt itchy inside my dark blue suit.

Ms. McCusker broke into a grin when I walked through the door. Chet and Brian tilted their heads to one side, and Kate and Mary Lou giggled into their hands. Against the light pouring in through the window on the other side of the classroom I could see individual strands of hair floating away from their heads, waving softly between drifting swirls of dust. Tina was wearing a white dress, and her waist-length black hair was held by a bow made from the same material as the dress. A thin red ribbon went around her waist. She smiled at me as if I were sitting on a horse.

Class started and Ms. McCusker handed out colored construction paper and dull scissors. We cut out tracings of our hands and turned them into turkeys. We gave them dog and cat names, and while Ms. McCusker tacked them to the wall above the chalkboard, all the while talking about corn and Indians and Pilgrims, someone knocked on the door.

"Just a minute, class," Ms. McCusker said as she walked over to the door, opened it, and looked down at whoever had knocked.

"We're ready," a girl's voice said up to her.

"Okay," Ms. McCusker said, and looked back at the class. "Jin-Han, Tina, come over here, please."

Tina and I looked at each other, and felt everyone staring at us. Her eyes made me feel like I was giving something away. Then she stood up and with her back straight walked carefully over to Ms. McCusker. I knocked my scissors to the floor as I got up, put them back on the desk, and followed her.

Outside, a girl wearing faded bell-bottom jeans and a red hooded sweatshirt smiled up at us. A camera hung from a strap around her neck.

"Jin-Han, Tina, this is Stacey," Ms. McCusker said. "I want you to listen carefully to what she tells you and do exactly as she says. Okay?"

"Okay," Tina said.

"Jin-Han?"

"Huh?"

"Exactly as she says?"

"Okay."

"Good. I know you can."

We stepped down onto the gooey black asphalt and began following Stacey across the parking lot. "You guys are just the cutest things," she said, walking backward in front of us. She raised her camera and clicked a picture, then turned around again.

"Do you like my dress?" Tina asked.

"Oh, it's absolutely gorgeous," Stacey said without

looking back. I liked the way her hair flew in the wind. She seemed kind and ready to laugh.

"Jin-Han?"

"Huh?" I looked at Tina and immediately looked down at the passing black asphalt — pure relief from her dark, talking eyes.

"I asked you if you liked my dress."

"Oh," I said, watching the asphalt blur beneath my brown leather shoes. "I like it."

"Really? I like your suit."

"Okay," I said, feeling dizzy and confused, which was how I always felt around her, ever since we'd kissed each other.

"Here we are," Stacey said. We'd come to the side of the main school building: Up a few steps there was a red metal door under a short porch. "Okay," Stacey said. "Now Tina, I want you to come stand over here." She took hold of Tina's hand and led her up the steps. They turned around to face me, Stacey standing just behind Tina, the two of them flashing a double-decker smile. I had no idea what we were doing.

"Hmm," Stacey said, and tapped her finger on her chin. "Okay, Jin-Han, come over here."

I walked up the steps and stood next to her.

"Wait," she said, "I've got a better idea," and turned around and opened the red metal door behind us. "Come here, Jin-Han. Put your hand here and hold the door open."

I went over and did as she said.

"Now Tina, come stand here."

Tina came over and stood just in front of me. When she turned around I smelled a field of flowers.

Stacey stepped backward off the porch and smiled at us. Using her hand she moved us around some more. "Jin-Han," she said. "Move back a little, closer to the door — stop! There. Tina, step closer to Jin-Han." She giggled and said, "Perfect!" Then, after bringing the camera up to her face, she said, "Wisconsin."

"Cheese," Tina said brightly.

"Huh?" I said dimly.

Click went the camera.

Long after I'd forgotten about picture day, Ms. McCusker gave me a big red book with an eagle on the front cover. She said it was a yearbook, so I could always remember my time in kindergarten.

At home, we looked through the glossy pages and came across my class. Six little smiling faces in a row. Followed by larger pictures of us in our Thanksgiving Day costumes. (I was in a Pilgrim suit Ahpbah had made the night before out of string, poster board, and construction paper.) On the page before first grade there was a full-page shot of me, in my stiff blue suit and bow tie, holding the door open for Tina. On top of the page it said, CLASS SWEETHEARTS. Ahpbah and Uhmmah laughed and said how handsome I was. Tina, they said, was a very beautiful girl. We made such a good couple. At first I was embarrassed, but the more they kept laughing, the madder I became. And when I realized that my getting mad was only making Ahpbah and Uhmmah laugh more, I got up from the coffee table and stomped into my room. I took out my drawing pad and pressed a pencil into soft, thick paper. I drew a boat, climbed aboard, and forgot how mad I was.

MAKING
THE
KOREAN

A loud pounding on the door made me knock over the tallest stack of Lincoln Logs I'd ever built.

Uhmmah, drying her hands on her apron, came out of the kitchen. She told me I was making a mess and doing a poor job of keeping an eye on Jin-Soo, who was sitting on the floor in front of the TV watching the Bionic Woman run after a speeding getaway car. Uhmmah opened the door to Ahpbah smiling on the other side, holding two large rubber trash cans stacked on top of each other, the handle of a shovel jutting out of the top.

"Ahpbah!" Jin-Soo cried out happily, speed-crawling toward him. Uhmmah caught her on the way and swooped her up into her arms.

"What's that?" I asked.

"You'll see," Ahpbah said, sliding past Uhmmah, who shut the door behind him. "What's for dinner?"

"*Bibimbap*," Uhmmah said, coming over and setting Jin-Soo on the couch behind me. She told me to play with her as she headed back into the kitchen.

"Bibimbap!" Ahpbah repeated, carrying the trash cans through the living room to the door opening out onto our small, fenced-in back porch. "Jin-Han's favorite. You're a lucky boy to have a mother who loves you so much." He set the trash cans down, opened the door, picked the trash cans up, and went outside. I squeezed Jin-Soo's nose shut until she had to open her mouth to breathe. Ahpbah came back in a moment later, slapping his hands together.

Bibimbap was one of my favorite dishes because it was one of the easiest to eat — a big bowl of rice with bulgogi, spinach, bean sprouts, fried egg, and whatever else you wanted to throw in. Uhmmah mixed everything up for me, and then I ate it with a spoon, which I found a lot easier to use than chopsticks.

Every bite encouraged another.

After junyuk, Uhmmah put Jin-Soo in the baby walker and took her into the kitchen so she could watch over her as she started preparing a new batch of kimchi.

Ahpbah took me outside onto the back porch, where he started digging two large holes into the ground.

"What're you doing?" I asked.

"This is to make your uhmmah's life easier," he said, picking up one of the trash cans and pushing it down into one of the holes. It stopped about halfway. He pulled it back out and started digging again. "In Hangook we making kimchi and keeping it in the stone jars. It last a long time and tasting better that way. From so, so long ago we do it this way, to make sure we having food during the wintertime. We putting the salt on the cabbage and the pickles and the radish, and keeping it in the stone jars so we don't going hungry. And then we using khochujang because the salt, it's not so very easy to find long ago. Without the kimchi . . ." He laughed at a thought. "I guess you can saying kimchi making the Korean!"

"You're putting kimchi in the trash cans?"

"Yes." Ahpbah laughed again. "Kind of crazy, isn't it? But we don't having the stone jars here, and this will working actually maybe better. We putting it in the ground to keeping it cooler. The stone jars you don't have to. They keeping it cool above the ground. The best thing is this is so much bigger, so Uhmmah won't having to make kimchi all the time. She working hard every day and too, too tired when she coming home." He pulled himself out of the hole and slid one of the trash cans down into it. It fit perfectly.

"Ahpbah?"

"Yes, Jin-Han."

"Why did you leave Korea?"

"Why did I leaving Korea?" He stopped digging for a moment. "It was not so easy to living there. It was a very, very poor country that time. I think it's getting better now, but when I was a young man after the army, the future . . . it didn't looking so good for me. I had to living with my ahpbah's brother, your *kuhn* ahpbah, and his wife, because my ahpbah and uhmmah, your *hahrah-buhjee* and *hahlmuhnee*, dying when I was still very young. It was very hard time that time, and lots of people don't have the chance to living so long. Not like here. When I having a chance to leave . . . I hearing about a job in Germany . . . to do the coal mining. . . ."

"Coal mining?"

"Yes. I working under the ground with other Koreans. We all coming together from Korea and digging in the tunnels for the coal. It was a very, very hard work, but we making more money than if we stay in Korea. You seeing these arms?" He jabbed the shovel into the ground and raised his short, thick arms, flexing them like parentheses around his face. "It was so very hard and dangerous work, but I having to do it. And I starting to save money and going to university in Germany. And then I meeting your uhmmah." The other trash can slid into its hole snugly and Ahpbah clapped the dirt off his hands. He unfurled two trash bags he'd set aside and lined the trash cans. "And then she and I getting married. And after you were born, we deciding to come to this country. Everybody knows in America there is so much opportunity. Here we can making our own business easier. And then later you and Jin-Soo can going to university." He put the lids on the trash cans and stepped back from his work. "There!" he said, leaning on the handle of the shovel. His smile always made me smile. "Now we never running out of kimchi!"

We went into the apartment and told Uhmmah the trash cans were ready. "Good," she said, and washed her hands in the sink. She went over and lifted Jin-Soo out of the walker and set her onto my back, telling me not to drop her. Then she and Ahpbah picked up large bowls of kimchi she had prepared and we all walked out to the back porch.

Moths flittered about the yellow night-light above the door. Ahpbah set his bowl of kimchi down and removed the lid of one of the trash cans. Then he lifted the bowl and tipped the kimchi out into the lined trash can. It made a wet, sloppy sound like fish being dumped into buckets. Uhmmah poured in her batch of kimchi. We looked down into the trash can still mostly empty, the pungent odor of spicy, pickled cabbage rising up to us. I thought it was kind of gross, all that kimchi buried in dirt, but when I looked up at Ahpbah and Uhmmah, their eyes were far away.

Ahpbah put the lid back on. "Time to sleep," he said, reaching over my shoulder and pinching Jin-Soo on the cheek. "Tomorrow we going to work."

100 PERCENT
HUMAN
HAIR

I was behind the counter watching *Soul Train* on TV. Mr. Lee, the man who'd sold us the wig store, had told Uhmmah and Ahpbah to watch it to keep up with the latest fashions. I was supposed to be watching Jin-Soo, but she was just drinking from her bottle, sleeping, and drooling — boring compared to TV.

The bells on the front door rang, and we looked up to see an older black woman poke her head into the store. Uhmmah and Ahpbah stood up behind the counter and smiled at the woman as she looked around at the wigs on the shelves.

"Hello! Come on in!" Ahpbah said brightly.

The woman at the door frowned, looked behind her, and then walked in. She was wearing orange bell-bottoms and a white-and-red flower-print shirt with its tails tied into a knot over her belly button. She had a green bandana tied around her head, and her face shined from walking outside.

Ahpbah came out from behind the counter and walked toward her. "Can I helping you?" he asked with a smile. "You needing a wig today? As you can see," he turned and waved at the wigs on the walls, "we having all kinds."

"Yes," the woman said. "I need a wig. But I'm just looking right now."

"Sure, sure!" Ahpbah said, and he went to the front of the store, pretending to straighten things as he waited to jump to her assistance. Uhmmah stood quietly behind the counter and watched the woman move around the store. Her initial smile had turned into a thin, flat line. The customer wasn't exactly smiling, either, and kept squinting around the store as if she didn't trust what she saw.

She came to a stop in front of Uhmmah. "You got human-hair wigs?" she asked.

"Yes," Uhmmah said, looking the customer up and down. "Very expensive."

The woman pulled her head back and looked down her nose at Uhmmah. "You think I can't afford it?"

Uhmmah stiffened, and then asked Ahpbah in Korean what the customer had said.

Ahpbah hurried over, waving his arms, saying, "No, no! I'm sorry. My wife, her English not so good."

The woman looked at Ahpbah and asked him what Uhmmah had just said: "Why's she speaking Chinese? Talk English to me."

Ahpbah blinked at her. Then smiled. "Chinese? No, we are not the Chinese. We are Korean," he said. "She just asking me what you say." And then in Korean he told Uhmmah to bring down the human-hair wigs.

"She's not going to buy them," Uhmmah answered in Korean. "Look at her."

"What she say?" the woman demanded.

"Just get them!" Ahpbah said sharply to Uhmmah. And then in a different tone, he spoke to the customer in English. "My wife she getting the wigs for you now. You can see they have very, very good quality. You try them on, okay? Then you buying them!"

Uhmmah got up on a stepladder to reach the human-hair wigs. Most of the wigs in the store were made out of synthetics, which meant something that wasn't human hair. Next to the red-white-and-blue Afro there were three wigs on mannequin heads that had cards taped under their chins reading: 100% HUMAN HAIR. All three were straight and black. The shortest went down to the shoulders, the next was a little longer, and the third went down to the waist. (It was as long as Jin-Soo.) Ahpbah said no one ever bought them because they were too expensive. I thought maybe people didn't like not knowing whose hair they were wearing.

"Coming over here," Ahpbah said to the woman, walking over to one of the fitting areas and pulling a chair out for her. "Sitting down and trying them on, okay?"

The woman didn't respond, but went over and sat down on the chair. Uhmmah came over with the wigs, set them on a shelf under the mirror, and took the shortest wig off its mannequin head. She stood behind the customer and they glared at each other through the mirror.

"You take this off," Uhmmah said, gesturing at the woman's bandanna.

The woman's eyes shifted over to the reflection of me standing on a chair behind the counter. "Tell him to stop looking," she said, and I saw my face go red.

Uhmmah looked back at me and said, "Jin-Han." So I slipped off the chair and went down to the end of the counters, waited, and then peeked out from behind the corner in time to watch the woman carefully remove her bandanna. Underneath, she'd fixed her hair into small, even squares twisted into rubber-banded knots. Uhmmah stepped forward and slipped the wig onto the woman's head. After she stepped back, the woman turned her head left and right and looked at her reflection in the mirror. She ran her hand through the hair as if it were her own.

"I teasing your hair," Uhmmah said. "To make it looking more natural."

"No," the woman said. "This doesn't look right. Lemme try the other one." She pointed to the next longest wig.

"That one too long for you," Uhmmah said. "This looking the best."

"I know what I like and don't like," the woman said. "Let me try that one."

Uhmmah muttered in Korean to Ahpbah, who was standing in front of the counter, that the woman was just wasting their time.

"Speak English!" the woman said.

"She say she think the first one looking the best for you," Ahpbah said.

"Let me just try the other one," the woman insisted. But she didn't end up liking that one, either. I didn't think the straight, long hair looked right on her at all. I didn't understand why any of the women who bought wigs from us wore them at all. Why couldn't they just use their real hair? Especially when it was so hot out.

"I like this one," the woman said, standing up and tossing back the hair from the longest wig. "Yes, this looks nice. Can you tease my hair into this one?"

"This is very expensive," Uhmmah said. "You want to buy?"

"I know it's expensive," the woman said. "But if I like it maybe I'll buy it. Do you want my money or not?"

So Uhmmah pulled back the wig a little and tugged out some strands of the woman's real hair. These she mixed in with strands of the wig's hair and teased them together with a comb, so that just by looking it was hard to tell that the wig wasn't the woman's real hair.

Once she was done, the woman stood up and turned around, then looked at herself in as many angles as she could think of. She watched herself walk away from the mirror, then toward it. She bunched the hair behind her to see how it would look if she were to tie it behind her. "Yes," she said. "Uh-huh. This is nice."

"You liking?" Uhmmah asked. "You buying?"

"How much is it?"

"Ninety-nine ninety-nine. Very expensive."

"Ninety-nine ninety-nine!" the woman said. "Why's it so expensive? I seen wigs like this for half that!"

"Human hair!" Uhmmah retorted. "Human hair very expensive!"

"I know it's expensive," the woman said. "But ninety-nine ninety-nine!"

"Then you no buy," Uhmmah said, and reached for the wig. But the woman jerked her head away from Uhmmah's hand.

"I didn't say that. Let me see what I have." And then turning a little away from Uhmmah, and making sure Ahpbah couldn't see, she reached deep down the front of her shirt and pulled out a roll of cash bound together by a rubber band. She walked over to the counter where Ahpbah stood behind the register and began laying down the curled bills. Uhmmah stood next to her and watched her count the money.

"Fifty-five dollars," the woman finally said. "That's all I got. I'll take it for fifty-five dollars."

"Oh, no." Ahpbah laughed from behind the counter. "I'm sorry, we can no do that. We making no money if we do like that."

Uhmmah shook her head. "You no buy. I taking wig

now." Again she reached to pull the wig off the customer's head, but the woman ducked away. "Fifty-five dollars. You take that money and I'll take this."

"No!" Uhmmah said. She grabbed the money off the counter and thrust it toward the woman. "You take money! Leave wig!" The woman looked at the front door and Uhmmah quickly stepped in front of her. "You giving the wig here!"

"Fine!" the woman spat out, her eyes flashing. She grabbed her money from Uhmmah's hand and started walking toward the front door. Ahpbah brushed past me as he came from behind the counter. My heart was pounding. The woman shoved past Uhmmah and headed toward the door. Uhmmah reached out and grabbed the end of the wig and pulled. The woman grabbed it as it slid off and they stood there playing tug-of-wig. But with Ahpbah coming up, the woman knew she'd lost, so she let go and hurried toward the front door.

"You people!" she said. "I'm telling everyone not to come here!"

"You go!" Uhmmah yelled. "No coming back again!"

"Don't you worry!" the woman yelled back. "Don't you worry." Then before she reached the front door she suddenly swerved to the right and with a violent swipe of her arm sent a long-necked mannequin flying off the display case. It crashed into the shelves on the wall behind it, knocking several heads to the floor, their wigs fallen over their noses.

Jin-Soo started crying.

"*You go!*" Ahpbah thundered, pointing as he rushed forward, his face nearly purple. But the woman was already out the door, slamming it behind her in a violent clamor of bells.

Uhmmah and Ahpbah stood where they were, rigid except for their heaving backs.

I hurried over to Jin-Soo and stuck the bottle back in her mouth. "Shhh," I said. "Shhh." But I could hardly hear myself over the slamming of my heart.

ONLY
ME

After Jin-Soo started walking, she figured out that pointing a chubby little finger up at me and saying "Ohpbah" was the right thing to do. Uhmmah and Ahpbah oohed and aahed and acted mushy all over her, and then laughed when she pointed at the drawing I was working on and said "Ohpbah" again.

"No, Jin-Soo," I said. "That's a monkey. It's hanging from a tree."

"Ohpbah," she said again.

"Dummy," I said.

"Jin-Han," Ahpbah warned.

I grabbed my drawing and scowled off into my room. I was in a bad mood because I was in a new grade at a new school. I didn't know anybody, and everybody seemed to know one another. Plus, there were so many kids that I felt invisible, and sometimes stood by myself under the monkey bars during recess.

One day, during naptime in the classroom, I started leaning over in my seat as if I were looking closely at something on the floor. But there was nothing there. I was just thinking it was more fun than putting my forehead on my desk and closing my eyes, until I leaned too far and slipped and fell completely forward, banging the side of my face against the edge of my desk as it crashed over.

I stood up quickly and looked around the room, my mouth hanging open. Everyone looked back at me with the same expression.

"Jin-Han!" Ms. Burgess said, standing in surprise behind her desk. She rushed forward and picked up my desk, and then knelt down in front of me. "You're bleeding." She turned the right side of my face up toward her, then grabbed me by the hand, stood up, and led me out of the classroom. "Class," she said as we walked toward the door. "Heads down and eyes closed. Naptime is not over."

But in a way it was, because after that I didn't feel so invisible anymore. I made some friends, and during lunch we compared our lunch boxes decorated with favorite TV shows. Chris showed off his new bicentennial quarters to me, and Jeff, this skinny guy who grossed everyone out by slithering the tip of his long tongue up until it reached the tip of his nose, once gave me half his ice-cream sandwich.

When the school year ended, Jin-Soo and I started going to a baby-sitter. Her name was Gretchen. The Paks dropped off James and Margaret there, too. Won-Hee and her family had moved down to Texas because business was better there. There were about a dozen other kids I didn't know from the neighborhood.

We all stayed in a big one-story house near the bottom of a hill, with a long backyard that sloped down into a ditch. While Gretchen made peanut butter and jelly sandwiches in the kitchen, the older kids went out into the backyard. The girls spent their time pretending to be even older; the boys worked at giving their uhmmahs more laundry to do.

One day James and the other boys came up to me with a plan.

"Jin-Han," James said, setting his hands on his hips. "We need your help."

"Uh-huh," I said, trying to shake off a Tonka dump truck wedged onto my foot. (I'd been using it like a roller skate.)

"You see that hole over there?" James pointed at the

small square opening leading into the crawl space under the house.

"Uh-huh."

"That's where we want to go."

"You're not supposed to."

"We know, Jin-Han. That's why we need your help."

"How?"

James turned around and looked down toward the ditch. "We need you to go down there and make a lot of noise, like you're playing with us. Like we're all down there. If Gretchen comes out looking for us, tell her we're with you."

I gazed down at the ditch and then back up at the house. I could see the shadow of Gretchen's head through the kitchen window. "I don't know," I said.

"Look," James said. "Don't worry. You probably won't have to do anything. We'll be done before Gretchen comes out."

I bit my bottom lip and looked down at the ditch again. "How long did you say?"

"Not long. We're just gonna go in real fast, look around, and then come out. Come on, Jin-Han."

"Well . . . ," I said, feeling trapped into doing something I didn't want to do.

"All right, Jin-Han!" James said, clapping me on the shoulder and looking back at the other guys. "See," he said. "I told you he would."

"Yeah, cool," they said, and started casually drifting toward the side of the house. James waved at me to go into the ditch, and I turned around and trudged down the hill. I found it hard to breathe because I didn't think this was going to work and I didn't want to get in trouble.

Down in the ditch I kicked around some dirt and rocks and sticks. It had been hot for a while, so everything was dry and dusty. I looked up at the house and hoped Gretchen wouldn't come out. It was blaringly quiet. The girls had gone inside, probably because they didn't want to be around when the boys, who seemed like they'd been under the house a long time already, got in trouble.

And then the screen door swung open and Gretchen stepped out. "Boys!" she called, shading her eyes with a hand. "Time for lunch!"

I'd ducked as soon as I'd heard the screen door catch against the jamb, and now stood up so Gretchen could see my head down in the ditch.

"Jin-Han? What're you doing down there?"

"We're just hanging out," I shouted up to her.

"Where are the rest of the boys?"

"They're down here, too," I said, staring dumbly at the dirt around my feet. "We're just digging and stuff."

"The boys are down there with you?"

"They're, uh . . . We're playing cowboys and Indians."

"Tell them to stand up."

"Who?"

"The cowboys and Indians."

"Oh."

She took a few steps down toward me and plainly saw there was no one else in the ditch.

"Jin-Han . . . ?"

I hung my head and slowly walked back up the hill toward her, my legs getting heavier and heavier. It wasn't so much that I was afraid of being punished, because I knew I would be as soon as I saw James walk up to me with a plan in his eyes, but it was more that I hadn't listened to myself. I should have said, "No," but I didn't. If I was going to get in trouble, I had only me to blame.

Covered in dust and dirt, the boys filed out from under the house and marched right into the living room and lay down on the floor. No PB&J for them, just straight to naptime.

The big surprise was that Gretchen didn't get upset with me. She understood that I'd been put up to being the lookout, and so I sat in the kitchen alone with her and ate my PB&J with a tall glass of chocolate milk. The whole time I tried to ignore James shooting angry eyes at me from the shadowy dimness of the living room floor, my feet kicking faster and faster under the table.

When I was done with my PB&J, Gretchen told me to stay put, that she had something special for me, and that I had to close my eyes.

It seemed like my eyes were closed forever, especially when I could hear shuffling and tiny whisperings gathering around me. I felt someone move close by and then caught a whiff of something sweet and sugary.

"You can open your eyes now, Jin-Han."

The first thing I saw was a round blue cake with white edges. I counted seven candles around green letters saying, HAPPY BIRTHDAY JIN-HAN! Then everyone else, even the boys who'd gotten in trouble for crawling under the house, started singing "Happy Birthday" to me.

Someone slipped a birthday hat on my head, and I looked up to see Uhmmah smiling down at me. I couldn't believe she and Gretchen had secretly planned this party. After a blinding flash I saw Gretchen looking through a black rectangular camera. I got two slices of cake.

I even won the game where you stood on a chair and dropped pennies into a jar. Nobody else could figure out you had to close one eye to make it work. My prize was a Frisbee. When we got home, Ahpbah tried to teach me how to throw it, but it got dark too soon and we had to go in. The last thing I got for my birthday was a blister on my thumb.

NEW SKY

Usually the smell of junyuk made me want to shovel it inside my stomach, but after PB&J, chocolate milk, two slices of cake, and a lesson in Frisbee-throwing, I felt like putting my stomach up on the table. Jin-Soo whined and complained about the food, because she didn't like the taste of fish. Ahpbah and Uhmmah stabbed at their food with their chopsticks, their voices growing harder and angrier.

"Yes, it was," Ahpbah said, bringing his spoon to his mouth and slurping loudly. "This was the best chance for us to make money. With our English we could never make the kind of money we need to make if we worked for someone else. We have two children now. We need to send them to good schools."

"But we're not making more money!" Uhmmah

pointed out, taking a spoonful of rice soup and blowing on it. Once it was cool enough, she brought it to Jin-Soo's lips and dripped it into her mouth. "We're losing the money we saved and borrowed from the Paks and the Shins. And the Shins left because they were losing money, too."

"I know," Ahpbah said. "I know. We didn't know enough about Memphis. We didn't know how bad it was here. Mr. Lee didn't tell us everything when he sold us the store. It's too poor here. Nobody has any money."

"We should never have —"

"Yes!" Ahpbah said, rising into one of his tempers. "We have to have our own business if we want to have a chance here! Maybe it won't happen in Memphis. That's why I visited the Shins in Texas. The money's much better there. They've got oil. Everybody's making money from oil."

"Oil?" Uhmmah said. "So we're going to make money from oil now? How are we going to do that?"

"Aigoo!" Ahpbah said, meaning did he have to spell everything out to her? "We're not making money straight from oil. We're making money from the people who make money from oil, which is everyone in Houston. It's a boomtown! The oilman makes a lot of money, so he buys a lot of things. Everyone he buys something from has more money, so they buy more things. If we just go there money will fall into our laps!" His hands were in the air, like a conductor leading his orchestra.

"Aigoo," Uhmmah said back to him, shaking her head. "Keep your voice down." She chopsticked some rice onto a leaf of lettuce, then a piece of *kahlbi*, a dollop of khochujang, and some kimchi. She folded the leaf closed and brought it to her mouth. "And what are we going to sell them? Wigs?" She yawned her mouth open and diligently worked the stuffed lettuce into her mouth.

"Yes!" Ahpbah said, working on his own bed of lettuce. "Wigs! There are lots of black people in Houston, and they have money, too. Not like here." He stuffed his mouth with stuffed lettuce.

I put down my fork and laid the side of my face down next to my bowl of rice.

"What's wrong, Jin-Han?" Uhmmah asked. "Are you sick?" She leaned over and placed the back of her hand against my forehead. "Go lie down on the couch."

I slid out of my seat and dragged myself into the living room. I collapsed onto the couch and curled around my stomach. Ahpbah and Uhmmah grew angrier and angrier, taking turns spitting out what each thought was

95

the best thing to do for the family. Ahpbah banged the table to get his point across, rattling silverware. Uhmmah said he didn't have to shout, which made him angrier. Jin-Soo started crying. I closed my eyes and moaned and hoped it would all go away.

Later that year, a truck even longer than the one we moved to Memphis with showed up outside our apartment. Two men in overalls hopped out of the cab and opened the large side doors. Inside there were already fixtures and display cases I recognized from the wig store.

Everything in our apartment was packed and ready to go. The men moved back and forth, filling up the truck slowly but steadily. Ahpbah occasionally helped them, chatting them up when he wasn't. Uhmmah wondered if he was just getting in their way.

We hadn't been in Memphis long, but we had a lot more stuff than when we'd left Chicago. I was impressed we had to have an eighteen-wheeler carry it all.

Once the men were done, we got in our car and followed them as far as the highway. After I made Ahpbah race them for a while, we soon lost sight of each other. Jin-Soo and I sat in the back, cozy in our makeshift traveling bedroom of pillows, blankets, and important toys we saved from the moving truck. The four of us sang Elvis songs and songs Ahpbah had taught us. My favorites were "You Are My Sunshine" and "Que Sera, Sera." They had stories I could see in my head when we sang them. Of course I changed the little girl in "Que Sera, Sera" to a little boy. Sometimes I tried to sing in time to the swings of the two small wooden masks hanging from the rearview mirror. One was a man's face laughing, and the other a woman's. Ahpbah had told me that many, many years ago in Korea, masks like that were worn by actors performing in villages throughout the country. Our *eemoh*, Uhmmah's sister, whom I'd never met, had sent it to us from Korea. I told Jin-Soo to watch the masks swing back and forth and front and back, but she said it made her feel sick, which was why I'd told her to do it in the first place.

When we started to get hungry, Uhmmah passed around a container of *kimbap*, another one of my favorites, especially since I could eat it with my fingers. Uhmmah and Ahpbah complained about not having any kimchi to eat with their kimbap. And then Uhmmah suddenly brought her hand up to her forehead, remembering . . . "Ominah!" she said.

"What?" Ahpbah said, startled. He straightened up and checked the mirrors. "What's wrong?"

"We left the kimchi!"

"What? The kimchi?" Ahpbah glanced at Uhmmah, and then suddenly laughed. "Ominah! Not the kimchi we put in the ground!"

Uhmmah laughed, too. "Yes! How could we have forgotten? What're they going to think when they find it? They won't know what it is. They'll never have seen — or *smelled* — anything like it."

"So much kimchi," Ahpbah said, shaking his head and laughing. "We couldn't have taken it with us, anyway."

"Still," Uhmmah said. "Such a waste. All that kimchi. We could have given it to the Paks."

"Oh, well," Ahpbah said. "We can't really do anything about it now, can we? *Que sera, sera* — right, Jin-Han?" He looked at me in the rearview mirror. "Whatever will be, will be!"

"Uh-huh," I said, and leaned back against the pillow to stare up at the night sky through the side window. I was full and tired and sick of being in the car.

Jin-Soo started whining, and Uhmmah looked back to ask her what was wrong. I kept staring out the window.

"Jin-Soo," Uhmmah said. "Why don't you play with your doll?" Which turned out to be the wrong thing to say. Jin-Soo started crying, "Doll! Doll! Doll!" while beating her hands against the seat.

"Where's your doll?" Uhmmah said, and twisted further to look for it in the backseat. "Jin-Han, where's Jin-Soo's doll? Will you find it for her?"

"I don't know where it is," I said grumpily, and squeezed myself deeper into my pillow.

"Jin-Han!" Ahpbah said sharply. "Don't talk that way. Sit up and find the doll."

Mad that I was suddenly being yelled at, I sat up and started moving blankets around and looking down at the floorboard and under the front seat all huffy-puffy. Finally I found it under my pillow where I'd hidden it earlier when Jin-Soo hadn't been paying attention. "Here's your stupid doll," I said, thrusting it at her.

She took it and then tried to hit me with it.

"Hey!" I said. "Jin-Soo tried to hit me!"

"Stop it, you two!" Uhmmah said. "Ahpbah's driving. Jin-Soo, come here. You're going to have to sit up front." Jin-Soo stood up, and I was only too happy to help push her headfirst over the front seat. Then I cleared the backseat and stretched out on my back. I hadn't planned it that way, but everything had worked out to my advantage. I felt the car thrum soothingly beneath me while the stars sprinkled the night above me. The street lamps . . . street lamps . . . street lamps . . .

Later, I opened my eyes to see the stars still out, glittering. Except for the highway badumping beneath me, the inside of the car was totally quiet. I sat up in the creaky vinyl and saw Ahpbah gazing ahead with one hand on top of the steering wheel. Uhmmah was sleeping with her head on a pillow against the window, Jin-Soo asleep in her arms.

When I looked out the side window, my jaw dropped. Off in the darkness it looked like stars were coming up out of the ground. I blinked and rubbed my eyes and realized what I was seeing were tall, spindly buildings massed tightly together, and sometimes tangled around one another — all of it decorated with white lights, some blinking. And then I noticed sudden bursts of blue flame shooting out of the tops of some of the buildings, and I realized I was looking at some sort of huge, sprawling factory, and that what I thought were buildings were actually pipes — hundreds, if not thousands, of all shapes and sizes lighting up the night sky. "Ahpbah?" I whispered.

"Hngh," he grunted, straightening up in his seat.

"What's that?"

"What's what?"

"That — over there."

He looked in the wrong direction at first, and then found what I was pointing at through the passenger-side window. "Ah!" he said. "That's the oil . . . the oil refinery."

"What's that?"

"It's where they making the oil to gas," he said. "So we can driving the cars."

"Oh," I said, though I wasn't sure what he meant. But I could tell it would be too hard for him to explain, and for me to understand even if he did. I knew he was thinking the same thing. It was easier to just ask him if he could see the jets of fire making candles of some of the pipes.

"Yes," he said, leaning over into Uhmmah's seat to see better. "Look at that. That is Houston. That is where the money coming from. Soon we will be making more money, too. And buying the house, and sending you and Jin-Soo to a better school."

Our voices had woken up Uhmmah and Jin-Soo. They looked out the window at the winking lights of the refinery rolling along with us. Uhmmah asked Ahpbah what it was and he explained it to her in Korean. I tried to follow along but gave up after a while. They were using too many words I didn't know.

In front of us the highway stretched on flat and endless, dark land on either side waiting for morning. I lay back down and gazed up at the real stars fading into a brightening new sky.

THE
CAPED
KOREAN

Uhmmah and Ahpbah had gone to work. I was in my underwear, Jin-Soo sitting next to me. We were on the couch watching Saturday morning cartoons, waiting for Mrs. Kim to come over and baby-sit us. The Kims lived in the same apartment complex we'd moved into, a sprawling three-story building centered by a swimming pool and laundry room. They were the first Korean family we met in Houston, and introduced us to the Korean church they went to, where we met more Koreans.

A sharp rapping on the window nearly gave me a heart attack. I looked over at the window and saw shadowy shapes on the other side of the drapes. Something told me it wasn't Mrs. Kim and, like the racing of my heart, I tried to ignore it. But whoever it was rapped again. I looked down at Jin-Soo and put my index finger up to my lips before she could make a sound. I stealthily slid off the couch and tiptoed over to the window. I went over to the edge of the drapes and tried to peek through the side without being seen, but there was no one there. Carefully, I pushed the drape aside and almost fell back onto my butt when Mrs. Kim's children, Jacob and Veronica, suddenly stuck their faces in front of me, all four of their eyelids flipped back pinkly. They burst into giggles and passed their hands over their faces to smooth their eyelids back down. "Open the door!" they demanded, and I thought about running to my room first and putting on some pants, but then thought if I just let them in right away, maybe they wouldn't think it was a big deal that I was in my underwear. I slid back the chain and let them in.

"You're still in your underwear," Veronica pointed out. She and Jacob jumped on the couch on either side of Jin-Soo. "Hey, Jin-Soo!" they said, and tickled her for a moment before turning their attention to the TV.

"Look! It's *Hong Kong Phooey*!" Jacob said. Penry Pooch had just jumped into a filing cabinet, and was trying to get out, transformed into number one superguy Hong Kong Phooey. Only a well-placed kick by his faithful cat, Spot, finally sprang him free. I ran back into my room and put on some pants. No one noticed the difference when I came back.

"Our uhmmah's coming up in a little bit," Veronica said. "Then we can go outside."

Jacob and Veronica stayed outside so much, they were tanned a roasted peanut color. Our uhmmahs and ahpbahs jokingly called them blacks in Korean. From behind, you couldn't tell them apart from the Mexican kids who lived in our complex. They loved to spend the hot, humid summer afternoons splashing around in the pool. It was almost like they were more comfortable in water than air. I liked to stay inside the air-conditioned apartment and watch TV and draw. I didn't know any of the other kids in our complex.

Even though Jacob was a year younger than me, in second grade, he was usually the one who led us around the apartment buildings. After his uhmmah had taken us to the convenience store once, where she'd bought us cap guns and plastic police badges, we ran around the floors of our building arresting people as they fumbled with their keys, groceries, and mail. Part of me felt shy about bothering these strangers, but most of the time they played along, raised their hands if they could, and said, "You got me."

Jacob never wanted to stop. Even after a long, grueling afternoon of strenuous police work, I could still hear his high-pitched, excited voice arresting more neighbors as I dragged myself home. Only when his ahpbah came out to smoke his after-work cigarette would Jacob's shift end. Running up to his ahpbah, he'd tell him he was breaking a law by smoking outside. "Put your hands in the air," he'd say, and his ahpbah would gaze out on the square of apartments and quietly puff his cigarette. Jacob would then grab on to his ahpbah's leg and try to take him in by force. At which point his ahpbah would drop his cigarette, stamp it out with his other foot, and then carry Jacob like a shin-guard into their apartment.

One day, Jacob showed up at my apartment with a long towel tied around his neck. He was also wearing Superman pajamas. I was wearing a red cowboy hat and matching cowboy vest and gun belt. My cap gun was fully loaded.

"Are you Superman?" I asked.

"Yes," he said, setting his fists on his hips and puffing out his chest.

Lightning fast, I drew my gun and fired BANG! BANG! BANG!

Something crashed to the floor in the kitchen.

"Jin-Han!" Uhmmah yelled.

Jacob smiled victoriously.

"Let's go," I said, and hurriedly shut the door.

Jacob took off running, his hands parting the air, the towel waving behind him.

I ran after him and fired a few more shots.

When we got to the stairwell we stopped to catch our breaths, then walked down to the second floor.

"So what else can you do?" I asked. "Can you see through walls? Can you fly?"

"Yes," he said. "I can see through anything except lead. And I can fly. See my cape?"

"You can't fly," I said. "That's a towel."

"It's a cape," he said. "It's a towel if I'm drying myself down by the pool," which he stopped to point at. "It's a cape when I have it around my neck and I'm wearing my Superman suit."

"Okay," I said. "Then fly."

"I will," he said, and we looked out over the pool. It was the middle of a hot, Saturday afternoon, not a cloud in the sky. It seemed like all the kids in the complex were crammed into the water, and just as many parents lounged around the pool on beach chairs drinking sweaty, clinking glasses of iced tea.

"Fly over and land by the pool," I said. "Can you do that?"

"What do you think," he said, and then started to climb over the second-floor railing.

"What're you doing?"

"Getting ready to fly. I have to get in position."

"Hey," I said. "I was kidding. You don't have to fly. . . . You *can't* fly."

"Yes I can," he said, and before I could stop him, he jumped.

And the crazy thing was, for a second — maybe less — he was actually flying. I saw it with my own eyes. For one blinkless moment he was stuck in air, the cape spread out magnificently behind him.

And then he landed badly, with a sickening thud, which half the people in the swimming pool heard. Amazingly he only ended up breaking his arm, but nearly broke his face trying not to cry. The next time I saw him I signed his cast.

THE OTHER
SIDE OF
THE STREET

Martin Luther King Boulevard was one of the widest and longest streets I'd ever seen. Split by a drainage ditch that ran for most of its length, the street went though an endless neighborhood of one-story houses and yards showing more dirt than grass. All the people who lived in the houses, and drove the cars, and patronized the stores in the neighborhood were black. A lot of them had Cadillacs, and spent their afternoons polishing them. Sometimes they gathered together in the corner of a parking lot and talked to one another perched on the front of their hoods. If they happened to see us drive past, their eyes followed us as far as their necks would let them.

Almost every block had a strip mall. Laundromat, BBQ, TV repair, pawn shop, fried chicken, shoe repair, record store, barbershop, and even a couple of Chinese restaurants. People parked their cars, got out and wiped their brows, then made sure they didn't move too fast getting into air-conditioning. Only one strip mall had a wig store, and we parked in front of it. On one side was Chet's Chitlins, on the other a shoe repair. Next to the shoe repair was a Laundromat.

We got out of the station wagon and I helped Ahpbah pull out the large flat pieces of wood we'd just gotten at the lumberyard. We carried them into the back of the store, where Ahpbah started marking up the white sides of the boards with all kinds of lines and curves. Then he had me hold one end of the board while he cut along the lines and curves with an electric saw. Letters fell to the floor.

Out in front of the store he leaned a metal ladder up against the wall and told me to hold on to the bottom. Taking a drill up to the top, he began carrying the letters up one by one and attaching them to the strip of corrugated metal running along the top of the wall. Once he drilled in the last screw and came down the ladder, we stepped back into the parking lot, behind the station wagon, and read what he'd put up: ROSA'S WIGS. I was impressed. I didn't know he could do that.

"Who's Rosa?" I asked.

Ahpbah laughed. "Your uhmmah! Don't you know that?"

I didn't. I was ten years old and it was the first time I'd heard about Uhmmah having an American name. I'd seen her Korean name, Chung-Sil, on some papers in the drawer where we kept our green cards, but I never knew she had an American name. To me and Jin-Soo she was just Uhmmah.

"Do *you* have an American name?" I asked.

"Of course," Ahpbah said. "Philip."

"Philip? What about me? Does Jin-Soo have one?"

"No, not yet. We thinking if you wanting one later, you can choosing your own."

"Really?" But before I could think of a list of possible names, he brought the ladder down on its side and told me to grab the other end. As we lifted the ladder and started walking, a black boy ran up to me, his tongue bright red from the bottle of cherry soda he was holding in one hand. *"Ching, ching chow ching!"* he blurted, and then broke into a laugh and ran back toward his mother sitting on one of the yellow plastic chairs outside the Laundromat. "Tyrone!" she yelled, slapping at him with the pink flip-flop she'd been fanning herself with. "Leave those people alone!" He ducked with a giggle and scurried into the Laundromat, where he looked back at me through the window. My face was red and my heart suddenly fast. My knees felt shaky and I wanted to go back into the store. The hard edges of the ladder dug into my hand.

Ahpbah laughed and said in Korean, "What a silly boy." But I didn't think it was funny at all, and I got mad at him for thinking it was. Didn't he understand what had happened? It didn't make sense to me that people who didn't want to be treated differently because of their color could turn around and do the same thing to other people. On the other hand, I knew I wasn't any different. At school, there had been a new girl in our class from Pakistan. She had long, shiny black hair like an Indian girl, but her skin was the color of eggplant. We never gave her a chance. She was left out or ignored for most of the year. And although I understood a little what she must have been going through, how bad she must have felt, I was afraid that if I stood up for her, it would remind all my classmates, who'd gotten used to me by now, that I might be different, too. She ended up not coming back the next year. Ahpbah jerked on the ladder and pulled me out of my thoughts. He opened the door and we stepped into the store.

Inside, Uhmmah was teasing wig hair into a woman's real hair, and telling another customer she'd be right with her. A third customer followed me in. "Yoboh," Uhmmah said, gripping a couple of bobby pins between her lips. "Can you hurry up? The customers are waiting." We took the ladder into the back, where Jin-Soo sat on a rug and watched a little portable black-and-white TV Ahpbah had bought. Occasionally she rocked the doll in her arms. All the mannequin heads on the shelves were bald.

I went over and sat down in front of my LEGO fort still in progress. I picked up a LEGO and thought about where I could put it, came up blank, and then threw it back in the box. I looked up and saw Jin-Soo happy in her world. So I went over and yanked the doll out of her hand.

Tyrone's uhmmah came into the store one day to buy a wig, and Ahpbah found out Tyrone made money by mowing lawns. He asked her if she thought her son wanted to make more money, and she said it depended on what Ahpbah had in mind. "I want him teaching Jin-Han to riding the bicycle," Ahpbah said. "I working here all day, so I don't having the time." She told Ahpbah she'd talk to Tyrone.

The next day Tyrone walked into the store and said his mom had sent him.

"Hello, Tyrone!" Ahpbah said, putting his hand out for a shake.

Tyrone looked down at the hand, then at Ahpbah, then me, then behind him, then back at the hand. After making some kind of decision, he slowly took his hand out from under his armpit and put it into Ahpbah's. He almost giggled when Ahpbah began shaking his hand up and down.

Ahpbah informed us that Tyrone was there to teach me how to ride the new bike I'd gotten for Christmas. (We brought it to the wig store hoping Ahpbah would have time, but business was so good, he never could. "Time is money," he kept saying.) Tyrone and I looked at each other, our faces surprised and doubtful. But then because it didn't seem like we had any choice, we went along with the plan. Over the next few weeks, after a whispered tip on how to keep my balance, followed by a running push, Tyrone helped me crash into one parked car after another, until I didn't.

Soon after that I spent my afternoons biking up and down parking lots, but only for a few blocks along the boulevard. I wasn't allowed to go beyond that, and I was too chicken to even want to. Beyond Martin Luther King Boulevard was a place I knew nothing about.

One day I couldn't find anybody to bike around with. Maybe it was too hot, the sun almost white with heat, but I was bored with my LEGOs, tired of looking at wigs, and sick of torturing my sister. Tyrone lived on the other side of the street. I'd never been to his house before, but I decided to see if I could get him to come out. Looking down the street, I waited for a break in the traffic, and then quickly walked my bike to the grassy ditch in the middle. I did the same thing on the other side, then walked my bike to the light blue house on the corner. I rolled up onto the yard, which was the greenest on the block, dropped the bike onto the grass, and walked toward the front door.

As I neared the porch, the screen door squeaked open, and I could almost sense Mrs. Galloway before I saw her large body step out. She looked down at me from on top of her large, billowy dress. "What're you doing, Jin-Han? You want Tyrone? He's not here right now. He went off with those Johnson boys and I don't know who else. They all went in there." She waved back into a sea of houses.

"Okay," I said. "Thanks." I picked up my bike and rolled it back to the edge of Martin Luther King Boulevard. As I waited for a break in traffic, I suddenly decided that I'd ignore Uhmmah's warning not to bike too far from the store, and go look for Tyrone. My breath quickened with excitement as I glanced at our store across the street, and then giving my bike a running start, I jumped on and plunged nervously into the neighborhood.

Right away I saw it wasn't very different from our own neighborhood on the other side of the city. All the houses were made out of the same pale brick and looked like mirror versions of one another. The white concrete sidewalks and driveways almost glowed in the sun's burning heat. I could hear crickets and other insects calling as I slowly biked through. A gleaming, burgundy Cadillac turned onto the street and like a boat went past me. I could see myself in the sunglasses the driver was wearing, a toothpick working between his lips.

I turned onto a street that had a wooden fence running along the entire right side. In front of it was a ditch, and across the street was a large, overgrown field, barren except for the remains of a couch and the burned-out hull of a car.

About halfway down the block was a group of six or seven black kids looking at something down in the ditch. I rode up slowly and saw Tyrone. I stopped, got off the bike, put the kickstand down, and walked over. No one seemed to notice.

A dead dog was down in the ditch — a German shepherd on its side. The whole middle section was split open, a pinkish red meat, like the inside of your mouth, feeding a writhing swarm of black flies. Then the smell hit me and I stepped back.

One of the kids had a long stick and he climbed down the ditch a little to poke at the dog's face, its jaw stuck open and its black tongue sticking out. Nothing happened, so he stuck the stick into the open side of the dog, and the flies rose in a cloud of sudden buzzing. We all stepped back.

Still no one said anything. I looked over at Tyrone, but he didn't see me. He couldn't seem to take his eyes off the dog.

"Tyrone," I said. "Hey."

"Huh?" He looked down at me as if he didn't see me, and then back at the dog. Another kid gave me a look, glanced up at Tyrone, and then went back to looking at the dog, too.

I stayed there for a little while and kept glancing up at the side of Tyrone's face, but he never turned back to me. He was acting like he didn't know me. Another kid picked up a rock and pitched it underhanded into the dog's side. The flies went crazy and then resettled.

After a while I went back to my bike and got on. I looked back at Tyrone once more, but he was still looking down at the dog. I kicked the pedals into position, just like he'd taught me, and rode back to the store.

There were about six police cars in the parking lot when I got back, some of them with their sirens flashing silently. As I walked my bike up, four of them pulled away. The two that were left were in front of our store.

I stopped for a second and then hurried forward. Inside, Ahpbah was standing with one hand against the counter, the other on his forehead, talking to the large black police officer checking off boxes on his clipboard.

Uhmmah was sitting on a chair, tightly clutching

Jin-Soo's hand and shaking her head, "Aigoo, aigoo, aigoo . . ." She saw me and said, "Jin-Han! Come here! Where did you go?" I went over and she grabbed me by the hand. "Aigoo!" she said again, still shaking her head. She took a big breath and sighed, patting her chest. "Oh, my heart. How could this happen?"

A customer I recognized was talking to another police officer. I heard her describing a man who'd come in and pointed a gun around. He'd taken her watch and then made Rosa take all the money out of the register.

"Rosa?" the officer said.

"Yes. Rosa," the woman said, and pointed at Uhmmah.

I watched another officer dust for fingerprints, and saw for the first time how dusting for fingerprints was really a messy thing to do, not like on the cop shows. It got black powder everywhere.

After the police left, Ahpbah thanked the customer who'd been in the store when the man with the gun had come in. "Well," she said. "There's bad people everywhere. At least we didn't get killed."

We closed the store early.

The next day Uhmmah and Ahpbah came back at the usual time.

THE
TREE OF
LIFE

I was the best drawer in fifth grade, so Mrs. White picked me out to draw the Tree of Life. It was a big project, and I didn't know if I could do it. Unlike what I doodled on my book covers, which were things that just popped into my head, like cars with engines tearing out of their hoods, robots, or muscular arms and legs, Mrs. White wanted me to draw a huge poster-sized tree, and then show, in different levels going up the trunk, where plants were in relation to bugs in relation to animals in relation to humans in relation to God. I'd never drawn anything that had a story to it, and wasn't sure I could. But I got to work on it at the back of the room while the rest of the class took vocabulary quizzes.

During lunch, Joe Dimitris asked me if he could sit next to me. I nodded he could. He was new to the school and had thick, curly-wavy brown hair — the same color as the mole near the bottom of his right cheek. He set his rubber green coin holder next to his beige food tray, which had a corn dog in the main square, green beans in the small square next to it, chocolate pudding above that, baked beans, and finally a small carton of chocolate milk.

"I like your drawings," he said, using his teeth to tear open a mustard packet. He squeezed the bright yellow paste along the golden-brown corn dog. "Can you draw Spiderman? Darth Vader?"

"Darth what?" I said, feeling the vague queasiness I always got about halfway through eating a corn dog. "Darth who?"

"Darth *Vader*," he said. "Haven't you heard of Darth Vader?"

"No," I said. "I don't think so. What is it?"

"Not it — *who*. Darth Vader uses the dark side of the Force? He's controlled by the Emperor, who the Rebels are trying to destroy? Luke Skywalker? Princess Leia? R2D2? Haven't you seen *Star Wars*?"

"Nope," I said, tipping my milk carton to get the last bit of chocolate flavor up my straw, sucking air more than anything.

"You haven't seen *Star Wars*?"

"Nuh-uh."

"Well, what're you waiting for? Geez!" And he started telling me about a galaxy far, far away, where someone named Luke Skywalker got a holographic message from someone named Princess Leia, and how she was looking for some kind of knight called Obi-Wan Kenobi, who fought with something called a light saber. And on he went, telling me the story with sounds and acted-out battles and descriptions of strange planets and huge spaceships. I was so caught up in the story he was telling that when the bell signaling the end of lunch rang, I was shocked to find myself standing outside on planet Earth. He was that good of a storyteller.

When Ahpbah came home one day and said let's go see this thing called *Star Wars* he'd read about in the *Korean Journal,* I was almost disappointed by what I saw. It was also the first time my family had seen a movie together. We got there late and I had to sit on Ahpbah's lap in the back row, making the galaxy even farther away.

At the end of summer we went to visit the Shins in Austin. Uhmmah and Ahpbah were gossiping in the front of the station wagon. I couldn't understand what they were saying because they were using Korean words I didn't know. I kept beating Jin-Soo in thumb wrestling.

The Shins had a boy now, Sam, who I treated like a younger brother. Still, Won-Hee and Won-Soo always made sure he was never too far away from them, even though they sometimes teased him to the point of annoyance. Their hahlmuhnee had left Korea and now lived with them as well, because hahlmuhnees were supposed to live with their oldest son. She couldn't speak any English, but I liked her because she always smiled at me as if she knew exactly what I was thinking, and that she thought what I was thinking was smart and funny.

Jacob had *two* hahlmuhnees, though only one lived with his family. The other lived with his eemoh. Whenever the Korean New Year came around, the Kims had a houseful of hahlmuhnees, *gohmohs*, eemohs, *sahmche-uns*, *jahguhn* ahpbahs, and kuhn ahpbahs. Along with all his cousins, nieces, and nephews, Jacob bowed to each of these relatives and said in Korean, "*Seh hehbok mahnee bahdusehyoh*," which meant, "May you receive much good fortune in the new year." In return he'd get a five- or ten-dollar bill. On good years he ended up with a hundred dollars or more, though his uhmmah made him put most of it in a savings account. The rest he spent on video games down at 7-Eleven or Chuck E. Cheese.

I asked Uhmmah and Ahpbah why we didn't have any relatives like the Kims and the Shins.

"We do," Ahpbah said. "But they all living in Korea."

"How come they don't live here? How come all of Jacob's relatives didn't stay in Korea?"

"Who knows?" Ahpbah said, repeating himself by waving his hand in the air. "Everybody choosing their own life. We — me and your uhmmah — we choosing to leaving Hangook. But not everybody thinking that way. Some people they staying home all their lives, other people they leaving for something different."

"But I thought you said I didn't have any hahlmuhnees and hahrahbuhjees."

"Yah, that's true," he said, shaking his head.

"How come? What happened to them?"

He reached out and turned down Dolly Parton singing "Here You Come Again." I thought she had one of the sweetest voices I'd ever heard, and was a little disappointed we had to lower the volume. "I tell you before that time Korea was not so rich country, yah? Everybody poor. We don't eating well, and everybody health is bad. That's why *my* uhmmah, your hahlmuhnee, she dying when I was just a little older than your age now." He sat up and cleared his throat. "She had something in the chest. I don't know how to say it in English. And your hahrahbuhjee, my ahpbah, he was a shoemaker. What do they call it" — he snapped his fingers — "goddoggit! I don't re — *cobbler!*" he said, banging on the steering wheel. "He was a cobbler!"

"Aigoo," Uhmmah said. "Do you have to shout?"

"Yoboh," Ahpbah said. "I'm telling a story. *Chahmnah*. But before the war coming," he went on, "your hahrahbuhjee losing his business. The Japanese — they coming and they just taking everything. So my ahpbah now having to work for them. And he don't making as much money. And then the war coming, and the Japanese leaving, and the North Koreans, they coming down into Seoul, and everybody leaving the city. *Everybody*. So, so many people walking together. For three days we walking south, away from the North Koreans, until we meeting my uncle. Two weeks later your hahrahbuhjee die. It was too much for him. His health was not so good, and he was too weak. So my uncle having to raise me and my brothers and sisters. And he already having five children! It was a very, very hard time. And your uhmmah's . . ." He glanced over at her. "Her ahpbah and uhmmah dying when she was young, too." He reached out and patted her hand. "Right, Yoboh? What happened . . . ? Maybe you should tell them the story now? It's something they should know."

"Aigoo, aigoo . . . ," Uhmmah said, shifting around in her seat. "How can I tell this . . ." She reached down and brought out the thermos, and poured herself a cup of barley tea called *bohrheecha*. "I'm going to say it in Korean, and Ahpbah can explain what you don't understand, *ahruhsuh*? It's too hard for me to say it in English."

"Okay," I said, and tilted my head forward to concentrate.

"Aigoo," she said again. "I haven't told this in so long. But you should know this story. I never told you before because it's such a sad story." She shook her head and looked out at the road — or somewhere past it. "Your hahrahbuhjee was a very good man. He was very smart and handsome. We had a good life." She said her ahpbah was something I couldn't understand. She turned to Ahpbah and asked him if he could explain what she'd said.

"Architect," he said after thinking a moment. "Your uhmmah's ahpbah was like an architect — for the bridges. He design the bridges."

"Oh," I said, and pushed Jin-Soo's hand away from mine. We were both sitting forward with our heads sort of squeezed between the front seats.

"But then he died suddenly," Uhmmah went on. "We found out his health hadn't been so good. And Uhmmah, Ohpbah, and me . . . the money didn't last long. And then the war came, and that's when your hahlmuhnee died."

"What happened?"

"Oh, I can still see it so clearly," she said, shaking her head. "We went down to the village to buy some rice. Ohpbah — he was such a good, strong brother — was càrrying a bag of rice over his shoulder. I was in front, and Uhmmah was behind us. Everyone was going about their business. And then I noticed some people seemed to suddenly get excited about something, and then people started pointing up in the air, and then I realized the low buzzing sound I'd been hearing in the background was suddenly getting louder and louder. 'Run, Chung-Sil!' Ohpbah said, and I looked up behind us and saw a plane flying down toward us. *Bbahli! Bbahli!* Uhmmah shouted, waving her hands at us, and everyone started running and screaming. The plane was really loud now, and then it started shooting at us. It was a terrible sound. I could hear things falling and bursting apart behind me. I ran as fast as I could, and somehow, in all that noise, I realized there was more than one plane. I was screaming and running, and when it felt like the noise couldn't get any louder, I threw myself into an open doorway, my hands over my head. I looked back thinking Uhmmah and Ohpbah were right behind me, but they weren't! I went back to the door and looked out onto the street, and there they were, back almost where I'd started running. Uhmmah was down on her knees, crying and holding on to Ohpbah's arms. He looked like he was trying to get her to stand up, and then he threw the bag of rice down and knelt down and put Uhmmah onto his shoulders. When he stood up I saw a big red spot on the back of her *hanbok*. And then he ran with her over his shoulder. I stepped out of the doorway and called them over. 'Uhmmah! Ohpbah!' He saw me with tears coming down his face, and turned toward me, and I stepped to the side as they stumbled into the building. I ran in behind them, and Uhmmah was on the ground moaning, and saying, 'Aigoo! Aigoo! What will happen to you? Who will take care of you?' And she told Ohpbah to take care of me, and make sure I made a good life, and that I should always take care of my ohpbah. And Ohpbah and I were crying, telling her to stop saying these things . . . Aigoo." Uhmmah sniffed, and I swallowed the lump in my throat.

"Aigoo," Ahpbah said, and struck his hand against the steering wheel. "How could life be so hard sometimes."

"Yoboh. Life is always hard. We have to work to make it easy." Uhmmah sniffed again. "But she lived a few weeks more. She was strong and fought as long as she could. But we didn't have the kind of medicine and doctors we have here. That's why I became a nurse."

"Aigoo," Ahpbah said. "That's enough for now. We can talk about this more some other time. Jin-Soo needs to sleep now."

"Uhmmah," Jin-Soo whimpered, and pushed me aside. She squeezed up into the front and sat next to Uhmmah.

I sat back and looked out my side window. Ahpbah clicked off the radio. Eighteen-wheelers whooshed by. No one said anything. I climbed into the back of the station wagon and spread out on my back. At some point I fell asleep.

When we got back to Houston I had two new books waiting for me in the mailbox. It seemed like I'd been getting books in the mail for as long as I could remember. But I'd stopped reading them a while ago. There just wasn't a lot to read. Every page had a picture that I liked looking at, but I didn't find the words very interesting. There were only a few sentences on each page. I skimmed over them and then added them to the pile in my room.

Our new teacher at St. Thomas V, Sister Morata, took us to the school library once a week. The first several times no one seemed to know what to do. Sister Morata told us we had to pick a book, have the card that was tucked into the yellow pocket glued into the back of the book stamped, and return the book in a week. If we didn't, we had to pay three cents each day it was past due.

For a while I checked out books that looked like the ones I got at home, some of which the library had. But they were just as uninteresting. Then I noticed that some of the girls went to a specific group of shelves in the library and seemed to know what they were checking out. I'd recently figured out girls were different from boys in this way — not only had some of them started to wear bras, but almost all of them seemed to know about things without it having to be spelled out to them. They seemed to see things that weren't there, and say things without saying them. They were almost telepathic. Like some advanced race. And I learned early on that I got smarter by paying attention to them. Everybody else thought it was because I was Oriental and naturally brainy.

So I started looking at the shelves like I watched the girls do, and soon realized the books were grouped into different categories: books about places, books about people, books about animals, books about wars, books about girls, books about boys. Some had a few ink sketches in them and some had blurry black-and-white photographs on glossy paper in the middle of the book, but mostly they were filled with words — words that as I started to read them put worlds inside my head that sometimes seemed more real than the world I really lived in. It was better than watching TV. It was even better than listening to Joe Dimitris. It was as good as being there. It *was* being there.

Whatever I checked out, Marlene, the young librarian who sometimes got snippy with Sister Morata about letting us check out whatever we wanted, always seemed pleased with my selections. "Mmm," she'd say. "*A Wrinkle in Time.* That's a good one." And I'd smile and wait impatiently for school to end so I could start reading it in the car on the way to the wig store.

All around the blackboard at the front of our classroom were blue-inked mimeographs of the outline of America. There was one for each of us, our names at the top, and every time I finished a book, Sister Morata put a gold star on my America. Pretty soon I had the most stars in the class. Though it would've been nicer if Sister Morata had let me put the stars on myself; lick the minty glue on the back. If each of us had been able to stick the stars up ourselves, more of us might have read. But it was her first year teaching and she wasn't very good.

DAY OF REST

The door banged open and the light came on. I groaned and pulled my blankets over my head.

"Wake up!" Ahpbah said.

I could hear and smell breakfast being made in the kitchen. On Sundays it was usually a big pot of ramen with *mandu* dumplings added in if we were lucky. Just as I was sliding back into the blackness of sleep, Ahpbah rapped loudly on the door again.

"Wake up! We're going to be late."

"Nggggg," I groaned, and flopped onto my other side. Lately, waking up had become a kind of cruelty, almost torture. It was easier to just fall back asleep, but when Ahpbah suddenly grabbed the tip of my nose between his middle and index fingers, then squeezed the heck out of it, it was impossible.

"Yowwww!" I said, sounding like I had a cold, and was so mad at being woken up this way that I swiped blindly at his arm. But he caught my hand and dragged me off the bed. It was the most annoying way to be woken up, and I immediately felt a seething rage. At the same time, this was a weekly ritual, and I'd gotten used to it. I let my dead weight sag to the floor. If he was going to drag me out of my room, I wasn't going to make it any easier for him. Until the carpet burns became too much, and I started thrashing and flopping around until he had to let go of me. "Hurry up," he said, leaving me annoyingly wide awake on the floor.

Once we got to church, the priest, Father Kolba, who was actually a gray-haired Polish man who'd been a missionary in Korea, led us through an endless Mass using Korean that was different from what we used at home. It was the same Korean my parents used when talking to other parents and sometimes to each other. It was faster and full of words I didn't understand.

I always thought Father Kolba seemed lonely. Which maybe explained his incredibly long sermons.

I sat next to Jin-Soo between Uhmmah and Ahpbah

and daydreamed about Middle Earth, which I guessed was even older than the Old Testament, while Father Kolba said something something something, Amen. Until something something something it was finally over.

Amen.

But then before Father Kolba actually left the altar, some *ahjushi*, a friend of Ahpbah's, came up to the podium like he was really sorry, but something something something something, etc. Every once in a while he pointed to someone in one of the pews who stood up and bowed while everyone clapped. Sometimes the ahjushi said something that made the adults laugh. Father Kolba looked sleepy. Babies waaahed in the nursery room. Finally the ahjushi bowed and went back to his seat. Father Kolba said something something, Amen, and the organ and choir and everyone else who knew the words sang forth angelic somethings while Father Kolba and the altar boys marched slowly out the front doors.

Outside, the adults gathered in small clusters and shook hands, bowed and chatted and smoked and laughed. The smaller kids went crazy around them, chasing one another and hiding behind their ahpbahs' legs, while the older kids went off into their separate groups. Gradually the uhmmahs made their way into the gym, where some uhmmahs already were, preparing the big after-Mass buffet.

I was shy with the other kids because I only saw them once a week. And I didn't feel comfortable with the way they thought I'd automatically like them. I didn't feel because we were all Koreans we had to act like we'd known one another for years. Besides, they all liked to play baseball, football, or basketball, which I wasn't good at. None of them ever wanted to sit down and draw. Or read.

Jacob didn't have my problem. He got along with the other kids as well as he got along with me. And sometimes, like today, he talked me into shooting the basketball around with some of the boys. I wasn't any good, but at the same time I got into it, and ran for loose balls as fast as I could. Though I never stopped checking my new LED watch to see what time it was. I couldn't wait to get back in the car and rejoin Frodo's quest for the ring.

I looked over at the long tables where Uhmmah was sitting and saw Ahpbah and Jin-Soo with her. That meant it would be easier for me to get them to go home. So I told Jacob I'd be right back and went over to where they were sitting.

Even though Uhmmah wanted me to play with the other kids, she also knew how much I would rather sit in my room and read. So she started saying her good-byes and we went out to the car baking in the middle of the parking lot. Ahpbah started the car and flipped the air-conditioning to high. We stood outside the hot, steamy car with all the doors flung open and waited for it to become once again safe for humans. During the long drive home I sat in the back and read *The Fellowship of the Ring.* I could tell I liked a book if I chewed the tips of my fingers while I read it.

Ten minutes from home, Uhmmah pointed at the dreaded plant nursery by the side of the highway, and told Ahpbah we needed to get more topsoil. Which meant we had to walk around in the hot sun while Uhmmah bought some new plants to spruce up the lawn, along with heavy bags of soil and mulch. Which meant that instead of spending the rest of the afternoon sitting in the coolness of my bedroom reading Tolkien, I was going to be outside helping Uhmmah and Ahpbah with yard work — two of my least favorite words.

Sunday was the only day Uhmmah got to work on the house. The other six days of the week she sold wigs, in a place she was never comfortable being in. She had plenty of regular customers she'd gotten friendly with, but she always felt the neighborhood was a dangerous place to be, especially after the store had been robbed that time. When she came home she made dinner and did our laundry. Ahpbah had become a car salesman and was selling Pontiacs. He blow-dried his hair into a big, puffy pompadour.

With both of them working, we were able to buy a house and a piano, since Jin-Soo and I were taking lessons. Uhmmah was proud of the house. She'd come a long way from watching her uhmmah being shot down by a plane. She wanted the lawn to be the thickest and greenest on the block. She planted hedges around the house and rosebushes by the door. While Ahpbah mowed the lawn and I stuffed the cut grass into large plastic bags, Uhmmah repotted the plants inside the house. Then got on her hands and knees and polished the tile in the foyer. Then made dinner. And folded the laundry. And vacuumed. And complained about her aching feet, and her lower back. And told me to practice the piano.

It was how she rested.

SLOW DANCE

Lauren Paull was one of the most popular girls in junior high. One day she grabbed my Rubik's Cube out of my hand, and before I could stop her, she finished it for me. After that we spent a lot of time talking to each other, and I realized I could say things that could make her laugh. I really liked it when I made her laugh. Sometimes I spent all of lunch period trying to make her laugh, and never got around to hanging out with Joe, who I needed to talk to about our next Dungeons & Dragons game. Lauren had never seen *Star Wars*. Her family didn't even have a VCR.

Next weekend her parents were letting her host a dance at their house. I found out through a note she passed me during social studies. Everyone else found out when Mrs. Alper caught me reading it and made me stand up and announce it to class. "'My parents said we could have a dance at my house,'" I read aloud, trying not to smirk. I could feel everybody sit up out of their boredom, except for Mrs. Alper, who sighed like a tire deflating.

"Sit *down*, Jin-Han," she said.

Of course then everyone was confused and amazed that *I* was hosting a dance, until Lauren and I cleared things up during lunch.

It was in her garage. I wouldn't let Uhmmah get out of the car. I would've just asked her to slow down enough for me to jump out and roll onto the grass if I didn't think it would've dirtied my new shirt, which I'd nagged Uhmmah into letting me buy at the mall.

Inside the garage it was dark and cool. A disco ball hanging from the ceiling threw fat, blurry stars around the room. Some top-ten hit was playing on the stereo, and Mr. and Mrs. Paull greeted me and asked me if I wanted any punch.

"Is it spiked?" I asked.

"Oh, ho, ho!" they laughed. "You're such a funny boy, Jin-Han."

Lauren came up smiling, her lips glossy. "Nice shirt," she said. Her hair was pulled back in a ponytail, and I noticed her earrings were different colors. One was red and the other green. When I looked closer I saw they were pieces from a Rubik's Cube.

"Hey," I said. "Neat."

"Thank you for noticing, Jin-Han," she said.

"Aw shucks," I said, and then someone crashed into me from the side. I managed to stay on my feet, and looked up to see Joe tipping back a big black cowboy hat.

"Whoops," he said. "Sorry, pardner."

"Hey Joe," I said. "Nice hat." But he was already flailing away to a new song. His face was shiny and marked by a constellation of zits. Lauren went to say hi to Kelly Ford and Maria Lima.

Everyone began breaking up into little groups. No one was really dancing, just standing around talking and shifting from one foot to the other while sipping punch. Mr. and Mrs. Paull quietly slipped away. Lauren went around talking to everybody and making sure the punch bowl didn't run low. Then a slow song came on.

It was the first slow song of the night, and everybody kind of got quiet and squinted across the dark room at one another. This was what we'd come here for. I had my eye on Lisa Perec, Amanda DeLillo, and Maria Lima. But I looked at all the other girls, too.

Adam Guerrero was the first boy in our class to kiss a girl — Lucinda Mathews. How and where, I couldn't imagine, but after that he was the boy the rest of the boys looked up to. He just didn't seem to be afraid of girls, and seemed to know exactly what to do with them. So even though it hadn't been agreed on beforehand, we waited for him to put his punch down and go across the room to ask Sabrina Lem for the first dance of the night.

Every boy followed. I asked Lisa Perec. I held her close. The smell of her hair, the warmth of her body, and then the song ended. As a new one began, I walked up to Maria Lima and asked her if she wanted to dance. "Sure," she said with a smile, and we slipped into each other's arms and slowly turned and turned and turned to another slow song. She was a little taller and had that smell kids whose parents smoke have. It was heavenly, and I closed my eyes.

One slow song after another we played musical

partners, until at some point we just kept playing one song over and over again. It was just somehow understood that this song was the only song that could possibly capture the moment we had all slipped into. I'd already danced through it with Lucinda Mathews twice in a row. The first time I had my arms around her waist, and could feel a little bit of skin on her back between her shirt and jeans. The second time I moved my arm and felt a little bit more skin. All the little hairs on my body stood up. She was wearing perfume that seemed to be made just for me.

When the second dance ended, I stepped back a little and asked Lucinda if she wanted to dance again. I felt kind of sleepy and bold and careless. She looked up at me and smiled drowsily. "Sure," she said. Everyone else in the room turned shadowy. We stepped back together and held each other tight. A little into the song I put my hand right onto the skin on her back. Nothing happened, and my heart beat faster. As we turned ever so slowly around and around, I gradually began slipping my hand slowly up under her shirt until I had my whole hand pressed flatly on her incredibly soft, smooth skin. More and more I slid my hand up her back. I'd discovered a new country and I wanted to explore every silken inch of its geography. But I'd never been there before and I was nervous and unsure of what I was doing. I didn't know what I would find and how it would make me feel. My hand was blind but ecstatic.

When the song ended and we stepped apart, I knew not to ask her again. She went and stood with Lisa and Kelly and they looked over at me and said things I couldn't hear. But I guessed they were good things about how I wasn't just Jin-Han anymore, cute and smart and nice but not someone to go out with. I went back to Adam and Chad and Joe and they were all excited about how I'd put my hand up under Lucinda's shirt.

The dance ended a little while later, and we were all milling about outside, waiting for our parents to pick us up. Everything seemed shiny — the cars, the trees, the night air — and I couldn't feel the ground. I floated over to Lucinda and said bye to her. "See you Monday," she said, and got into her parents' car.

Uhmmah drove up and I got in. Lauren came running up and knocked on the window. I pressed the button and it slid down. "Hey," I said. "That was fun."

"Hi, Mrs. Park," she said. "You had a good time, Jin-Han?"

"Yeah," I said.

"Yeah," she said, mimicking me, and laughed. "Thanks for coming. I'll see you Monday."

As we drove off, Uhmmah asked me how it went. I said, "Good," then sat back and hoped she wouldn't ask me any more questions. I didn't want to come out of the place I was in.

At home I moved carefully. I took off my shirt and brought it up to my nose and smelled Lucinda's perfume. I lay in bed and slow danced the night over and over in my mind until I fell asleep.

On Monday, everyone was talking about where my hand had been, wondering what I would do next. I hadn't really thought I would do anything next.

"She likes you," Adam said. "You should ask her out."

"Yeah?" I looked over to where Lucinda was standing with some other girls, who kept stealing quick glances over at us. "I don't know."

"Dude!" Chad said. "She wants you to ask her out! C'mon!"

"She does?" I looked over at her again and caught her looking at me. We both turned away.

"Yeah, Jin-Han," Adam said. "C'mon. She's right there. Don't let this get away."

"I don't know, guys," I said, and really didn't think I could ask her out. I couldn't imagine what would happen if I did. Where would I take her out to? Was I supposed to take her to the movies? And did I actually think I could get Uhmmah or Ahpbah to drive me? We'd never talked about this kind of thing at home. All Uhmmah wanted me to do was study for the rest of my life. When I explained I didn't have any homework, or that I'd already finished it, she wouldn't listen to me. "You having to study all the time to make a success!" she insisted. "This is why I working so hard for you." It was the same thing all the time — study, study, study. Nothing about who my friends were, or even what I was reading. Definitely not who I had a crush on. I didn't even know if there was a Korean word for crush. All I wanted to do was make out with Lucinda Mathews. Or Maria Lima. Or whoever. But I didn't know how to go about it. And I couldn't talk to Uhmmah or Ahpbah for any kind of advice. We just didn't talk about things like that.

"Jin-Han?"

"Huh?"

"So? You gonna ask her out or what?"

"I'll think about it," I said, and that was all I ever did.

PRACTICE

"Uhmmah?"

We were sitting at the dining table. I was chopping onions in the onion chopper while Uhmmah got ready to make mandu.

"Mmm?"

"I think I want to quit piano."

She stopped pinching the dumpling she was closing. "Moh rah gooh? After all the time and money we put into it?"

"I know," I said. "But I want to stop now. I'm tired of doing it. I don't want to do it anymore."

"But why do you want to stop now? We've spent all that money on lessons. I work six days a week to send you and Jin-Soo to a good school. My feet are always sore. My back aches. I'm becoming an old woman too soon. You need to go to a good school and make lots of money so that I can stop working. It was your idea to start taking lessons, anyway, remember?"

"But I was too young then!" I said. "I didn't know what I was talking about."

"Aigoo," she said, shaking her head. She finished closing her mandu and set it on the tray of mandu that was ready to be boiled. She started on another one. "Are you finished with that yet?" I opened the onion chopper and showed her. She took it from me and spooned out the onions and kneaded it into the pork that went into the mandu.

"Okay?" I said.

"Be quiet!" she said. "Don't talk such nonsense."

"Uhmmah!" I said. "God!" And made a frustrated sound and rolled my eyes as I got up and went to my room.

I fell back onto my bed and picked up the latest book I was reading, *The Catcher in the Rye*. I'd seen an older kid at church reading it while Father Kolba went on with his usual somethings. If he thought it was worth getting caught reading it in church, I had to check it out. I wasn't halfway through it yet but I already felt the cold of New York like I'd lived there all my life. And though I didn't understand what exactly the narrator was so upset about, because every other word was a swear word, I *felt* like I knew what he was going through. It was partly why I wanted to quit piano lessons. I'd been doing it for almost eight years and hated having to practice every night. It meant more to Uhmmah than to me. I felt like it was one of the reasons why I'd chickened out with Lucinda. If I did regular things like other kids did, maybe I would've asked her out. Maybe Uhmmah would've understood how American kids went on dates and dropped us off at the movies, and in the middle of a big love scene I would've leaned over and kissed Lucinda like I could only imagine doing. Instead, I spent my days after school in the back of a wig store. Something nobody understood when I told them that was what my parents did — owned a wig store. Where finally, after years of thinking about it in the back of my mind, I took a bald mannequin head in my hands one day, wiped off her lips, and gently, slowly, practiced for the real thing.

CHEMISTRY

It was the first day back after Christmas break and we'd been assigned new lab partners. I was a little late because I'd made a few friends since the beginning of the first semester and got caught up talking to them in the hallway.

Inside the door, people were milling around the new seating chart on the wall. I waited until I could see that I was sitting with someone named Anne Grissom. I looked for my table — and there she was, a girl I recognized from my walk home. Her hair was brown and long and wedge-like in the front, buzzed in the back. There was a perkiness to her that told me she'd probably been the first person to get to lab.

Suddenly I was feeling nervous. When I got to the table she looked up and smiled. "Hi," she said, her blue eyes surprising me.

"Hi," I said, and climbed up on my stool.

"I'm Anne," she said, "but I go by Sue. You're Jin-Han?"

"Uh, yeah," I said, "hi," and for the rest of the period I tried to look at her without looking at her. It wasn't too hard because she seemed completely focused on what Mr. Youngren was saying, which to me sounded like what people sounded like when you listen to them from under water. Sue's arms were long and graceful with lots of freckles, but they ended in nervous fingers that seemed to tremble just to make me like them better.

Fifty-five minutes of cotton balls between my ears later, the bell rang. We slid off our stools and I realized she was about three inches taller than me.

"See ya," she said with a smile as she gathered up her stuff and walked toward the door.

By the time I'd cleared my throat she was halfway across the room.

The next week I got to lab first and was reading *The Stranger* when she sat down.

I looked up and said, "Hey."

She got up on her stool and looked down at my book. "Is that any good?"

I turned it over and back. "This?"

"Yeah."

"It's all right. Pretty . . . strange, I guess."

"Hah," she said. "Is that supposed to be funny?"

"Uh, no," I said. "Not really. It's about a guy who's mom died, and how he accidentally kills a guy on a beach a few days later. But he doesn't seem to care. It's weird. But I can't stop reading it."

"Hmm," she said. "Maybe I'll read it. It looks pretty short. I don't read fat books, anyway."

"Huh," I said, and fanned the pages back and forth between my thumbs. And then I realized, "Oh! You wanna borrow it?"

"Sure," she said. "When you're done."

"Okay," I said. "Except it's from the library. You can borrow it from them."

"Great," she said. "I'll do that. And then we can compare notes."

"Yeah," I said, and smiled back at her.

She ended up thinking the book was too depressing. "What's *wrong* with him?" she said, and gave me a mix tape she hoped would cheer me up.

It made me have a huge crush on her. When I told

Jacob while he was over with his family one night, he said I should make a copy of the tape in case something happened to it.

One Friday, Sue and I walked home together. When we got to the corner of her street, she asked me if I wanted to come over. "My parents won't be home till later," she said. "So it'll be, you know, we can relax."

"Come over?"

"Yeah. I don't know. I thought we could listen to some music. I can show you my pictures."

"Okay," I said. "Sure. That sounds great!" But suddenly I was confused and very nervous.

She smiled and I managed to smile back at her. We started walking quietly down the block, which seemed to stretch on forever. My mind was a roaring mush, and my legs felt like wet noodles. I didn't know if I could remember how to breathe. Something was about to happen and I didn't know what.

The Grissoms had an upright piano and we were sitting on the bench. I hadn't told her I knew how to play because I was afraid she'd ask me to. And I thought if I did, it would ruin the moment, especially since I'd quit over a year ago and had hardly played since. Plus, if I took my hands off my lap, I was afraid they'd start shaking so much, I'd have to run out of there like I was some sort of freak.

"Can you play?" I asked.

"'Chopsticks.' Know it?"

"Uh, sure," I said. "Doesn't everybody?"

"Uh, no," she said, and bumped me with her shoulders.

We looked at each other and giggled. I turned to the piano and looked through the music on the stand. Beethoven, Bach, Chopin.

"Hey," I said. "Elvis! 'Love Me Tender.'"

"Yeah," she said. "Hokey, isn't it?"

"I used to sing it all the time when I was a kid."

"And you're proud of this? It's my parents'. They love this song. I have to leave the house every time I hear them sing it together."

"It's not a bad song."

"Please."

I opened it and centered myself on the keyboard, which gave me a reason to press against Sue's body.

"Hey, you know how to play?"

"Maybe," I said, and started playing the chords.

"Hey! You *can* play! Cool!" She started singing the lyrics. She broke up into laughter and leaned sideways against me. My nose dipped into her hair. It was cool and smelled like shampoo.

"Watch it!" I said. "Pianist at play. Do you mind?"

She giggled and then cleared her throat and started singing again. After a while I joined her, and by the end we were really getting into it. Finally we stopped, both of us giggly and something else. It seemed hot all of a sudden.

"You're such a dork," she said.

"You started singing first."

"So — it doesn't mean you have to be so into it." She laughed and grabbed my arm and leaned her head on my shoulder. It surprised me and I couldn't stop myself from jerking back a little. She pulled her head away, but held on to my arm a little longer and gave me a smile that made me laugh and look away. Then she suddenly stood up and said, "Go sit on the couch. I'll be right back."

She sat down right next to me when she came back, her leg touching mine, her hip touching mine, her arm. She opened a photo album on my lap and started point-ing at baby pictures of her, of her younger sister, her parents when they were younger, her grandparents. I was afraid to turn my head because she was so close to me, her lips right there, a few inches above mine.

When we were done, she closed the photo album and

leaned across me to put it on the other side of the couch. I looked down at my lap. She sat back and put another album on it. And this was her cousin, and this was when they lived in Albany, and here was her dog Max, and that was her dad in front of the Corvette. Finally, after turning the last page, when she shut the album and leaned across me again, I grabbed her above the wrists as she was sitting back down. She froze, and looked down into me, where she could see my heart beating crazily. I looked up into her big blue eyes, feeling like I was about to shout, and then like a wave to sky, rose up and met her lips to mine.

As I disappeared into the moment, I thought about how all those years of practicing on the piano had come in handy, while kissing bald mannequin heads in the back of a wig store had only shown me what dried hair spray tasted like.

UNDERSTANDING THE WIG

I dropped Sue's hand when I realized the white station wagon in front of the school was ours.

"That's my dad," I said. "What's he doing here? *Man.* I gotta go. I'll see you tomorrow."

"No kiss?"

"Sue," I said, looking at her pouting with her hands on her hips. "My dad's right there."

"Fine," she said. "Don't ask me for one tomorrow."

"Sue, c'mon. I'll see you, okay?"

I waved back at her as I got to the car. Inside, Ahpbah asked me who that was.

"A friend," I said.

"Pretty girl," he said. "You liking American girls?"

"She's just a friend," I said.

"Okay," he said. "Okay."

We weren't going home.

"Where are we going?" I hoped it wasn't the wig store. I hated going there. I was sick of looking at wigs. Being at the store reminded me how different my life was from other kids'. But then I didn't really know anything about the lives of other kids, since I spent so much time at home reading. Or watching TV. Which was all I did when I went to the wig store, the reason I thought my life was different.

"The wig store," Ahpbah said. "We needing to go helping your uhmmah."

"Well how am I going to help? There's nothing for me to do there."

"Jin-Han," he said. "You're supposed to helping your family. . . ."

I rolled my eyes out the window. It was time for a lecture.

"Anyway, the reason I'm picking you up today," he said, and then sighed. "I'm afraid I'm having some bad news."

I looked over and said, "What?" I meant to say it meanly, but halfway through the word I noticed how tired he looked.

"Your uhmmah . . ." He shook his head slowly. "Your uhmmah has the cancer."

"*What?*" I jerked up out of my slouch. "*Cancer?* What do you mean?"

"Yes." He started hitting the steering wheel with the palm of his hand. "It's a complete surprise. I can't believe it myself. The doctors saying she has the stomach cancer."

"*Stomach* cancer?" I didn't know people could get it there.

"Yes," Ahpbah said, shaking his head again, and suddenly it made me angry. I didn't want to hear this kind of thing. I wanted to be mad at him for telling me something so incredibly crappy, especially when I was having the most incredible time with my first real girlfriend, but when I glanced over at him I couldn't believe how wrecked he looked. I almost lost my breath for a moment. "Well, what'd they say? I mean, will she be okay?"

"Yes, I think so. Of course," Ahpbah said. "The doctors saying we finding it early enough. They saying she has a ninety percent chance to . . . to . . . And the doctors in Houston . . ." He started hitting the steering wheel again. "Lucky for us they having some of the best doctors in the world here."

I slunk down in my seat and stared at the passing traffic. Ninety percent chance to what? I didn't want to know. I glanced over at Ahpbah and wished he wasn't there, or that I wasn't in the station wagon, or that I hadn't woken up at all today. I felt confused, and didn't know what to think.

"Really," Ahpbah said. "Right now we shouldn't having to worry so much. We having to trust the doctors. They know what they doing."

"Okay," I said. "You said ninety percent . . . ?"

"Yes!" Ahpbah said. "Ninety percent is very good! Everybody thinking so. And your uhmmah, she's a very strong woman. As you knowing. This is nothing. There is nobody like your uhmmah." He nodded to himself — then stopped. I think he'd forgotten I was there.

It was a few weeks later. Sue's dad had dropped us off at the mall. We saw a movie and then walked around after. I could tell she was thinking about something.

"You're way hotter than the girl who played Allie," I said, guessing. "Elizabeth what's-her-name."

She smiled her row of straight little white teeth and jumped over to hug me from behind. "Hey! Don't, hey!

Aw, c'mon . . ." But she'd already lifted me off the ground and set me back down. Then she snuggled her nose into my neck for a second before stepping away again.

"We have to talk, Jin-Han."

"What're we doing now?"

"No, I'm serious," she said. "C'mon." She grabbed my hand and led me to the food court. We weaved our way to an empty table and sat down across from each other.

She looked at me with her flawless clear blue eyes. I could tell she was about to tell me something bad.

"What?" I said. "What's going on?"

"Jin-Han . . ." She sucked her breath in while biting her bottom lip.

"What? What is it?"

"Jin-Han, I think we have to stop seeing each other."

"What?! What're you talking about? Why?"

"Because I think we're spending too much time together."

"That's a problem?"

"No!" she said, reaching across the table and grabbing my hands. Her pupils seemed to grow larger. "Yes! I mean . . ."

"What happened? Did I do something?"

"No!" she said, and then moaned and leaned across the table. "It's your mom. I think —"

"What about my mom? What's wrong?"

"She's *sick*, Jin-Han. I think you need to be spending more time with her."

I gaped at her as if she'd betrayed me. "Uh, hello?" I said. "There's a ninety percent chance she'll recover? Remember?" I thought she was using Uhmmah as an excuse to break up with me. But I didn't understand why. "Is this your idea?"

Her eyes stumbled. "My dad thinks —"

"Your dad?"

"My mom thinks — it doesn't matter," she said. "I think the same thing. I don't think it's right we're spending so much time together . . . when your mom's . . ."

"But why do we have to break up? Is there someone else? Why can't we just see less of each other?"

I took my hands out of hers and sat back in my seat, my arms crossed over my chest. I looked off to the side, but everything was blurry.

"Jin-Han . . ."

I looked back at her, and a big wet tear rolled down one side of my face. I blinked and the same thing happened on the other side, and then I was crying like a baby in the middle of the food court in front of my girlfriend who was dumping me. She came over to my side of the table and put her arms around me. "I'm sorry, Jin-Han," she said, and cried along with me.

A food court custodian came by and asked us if we were okay.

"Yes," I blubbered, and then before I knew what I was saying, I told him we'd just lost the state championship.

Sue snorted wetly, which made me almost spray-snort, and then we were both laughing hysterically. The custodian shook his head. "Kids," he said, sweeping a French fry into his dustpan.

A couple of months later, Uhmmah came home from the hospital. She'd been in chemotherapy, bombing her body with chemicals. It was supposed to make her better, and I was feeling relieved that everything was going to be fine. I was looking forward to getting back together with Sue.

But when Uhmmah slowly walked through the door, leaning on Ahpbah, I could hardly believe it was her. I'd never seen her eyes so hard and shiny. She had a tube going down her throat, and she looked like she could have a baby any moment, her stomach was sticking out so much. And then I figured out what was wrong: the wig on her head. It wasn't even a nice one. Nothing about it looked natural. It was more like a toupee. But then I realized she didn't have any hair to tease into it.

Jin-Soo ran up to her and took her hand. "Uhmmah," she sobbed, and laid her face against Uhmmah's arm. I stood where I was in the middle of the living room, unable to move. Uhmmah looked at me and quickly looked away, almost as if she was embarrassed, that she was letting me down, my sister, Ahpbah, the family. Even if I had known enough Korean, I don't think I would've been able to say what I felt.

Jin-Soo and I took turns sitting with her in the bedroom. All I could do was hold her hand, ask her if she needed anything, sit on the floor and read a book. When Jin-Soo came in, I went out into the living room and watched TV, whatever was on.

THE
STRANGER

Uhmmah died today. Or yesterday, I don't know. Ah-pbah called me from the hospital. I was asleep when it happened. "Your uhmmah," he said. "Your uhmmah . . ." I could barely stand the sounds he was making on the other end. "Mr. Kim is coming to pick you up. Bring Jin-Soo."

On the way there, Jin-Soo asked me if everything was okay.

"No," I said. "Uhmmah's . . ." I couldn't say it.

"What, Ohpbah?"

"She . . . Ahpbah said she died."

"She's dead?"

"Jin-Soo," Mr. Kim said. He cleared his throat and shifted in his seat. "Your uhmmah — she is going away. Now you having to live the right way for her. She giving her life for you and Jin-Han. You can never forgetting that."

I looked back at Jin-Soo and almost wished I hadn't. Her face glistened with tears as she hugged herself. I reached my arm back over the seat toward her. "Jin-Soo," I said. "Jin-Soo . . ."

"Ohpbah," she said in a kind of whining sob that spilled into open weeping. She sat forward and grabbed my arm and cried against it, wetting it with tears and runny snot.

I looked straight ahead and tried to keep my own tears from falling.

Ahpbah met us outside the room. He was serious in a way I'd never seen him before. I couldn't imagine he'd ever had a squeaky laugh. He took Mr. Kim's hand with both his hands and shook it, bowing and thanking Mr. Kim so much for his help. Then he turned to us and pulled us into his arms, both he and Jin-Soo weeping helplessly. There were too many people around I didn't know, and I didn't want to cry in front of them.

"Okay," he said after a while. "Jin-Han, Jin-Soo, we going in and saying hi to your uhmmah, okay?"

"What?" I said.

"Just saying hi to her and good-bye, okay?" Ahpbah said.

I didn't understand why he was talking about her as if she were still alive, but he opened the door and we went in after him.

The room was dark, the curtains drawn. I could see her lying on the bed. Still. Part of me was terrified of getting up close to her, part of me was curious. Ahpbah walked over to her and leaned against the bed and started talking to her. "Yoboh," he said, and he leaned down and kissed her. "Jin-Han and Jin-Soo are here. They want to say how much they love you. They want to see your beautiful face one more time."

Jin-Soo and I looked at each other. Was Ahpbah okay?

"Come over here," Ahpbah said, and I could barely breathe as we walked toward the bed.

She looked like she was sleeping — quietly, peacefully. But I knew she wasn't.

"Uhmmah," Jin-Soo sobbed, and started sliding to the floor. Ahpbah quickly caught her and pulled her up. "Uhmmah," she said louder and repeated it several times, sobbing pitifully into Ahpbah's chest. I stood there and felt like I was watching this on TV, like I wasn't really there. Jin-Soo suddenly tore herself away from Ahpbah and fell toward the bed. She grabbed Uhmmah's hand and sobbed, "Uhmmah, Uhmmah, Uhmmah" into it.

Something started happening to me as I stood there. The air coming into my lungs felt suddenly cleaner and more pure. I felt like I could see things past what was there. I was as light as a butterfly and deep as a tree. I was in a brand-new place, where I felt like I could understand what was happening. That it wouldn't bowl me over. That I could carry it with me forever.

Ahpbah pulled Jin-Soo away and told me to say something to Uhmmah.

I said I already did.

Then kiss her, he told me.

I gazed down at her for a long time. She really didn't look any different from when she was alive. I swallowed and leaned forward and kissed her forehead. She was as cold as the kitchen floor.

The worst part was the wake. All these people I didn't know showed up at our house. Two aunts came over from Korea. One looked exactly like Ahpbah, and the other exactly like Uhmmah. It was amazing to meet relatives for the first time. But still, I didn't want all those people there. I didn't want to have to share my loss with them.

In the living room, between the piano and the fireplace, was a small table with a framed picture of Uhmmah on it. Candles and sticks of incense burned in front of the picture. As people came in, they went up to the little shrine and knelt down in front of it and bowed several times.

I felt like a fake when I did it. Ahpbah acted like I would know what to do. Which was crazy. I had no idea we did things like that. And suddenly, I had to do it front of a bunch of strangers? Still, I did it. There were too many people and I didn't feel like I could say no. And Jin-Soo had already done it. So I did it, as strange as it felt. My aunts sobbed loudly. I thought maybe they were overdoing it. But when we buried her, Ahpbah threw himself on the coffin and practically howled with grief, and I understood that was how Koreans did it.

FINDING
MY
HAT

It was a spur-of-the-moment kind of thing. I was sitting at home, flipping through the channels, unable to focus my attention on anything. Jin-Soo was at a volleyball game, and Ahpbah was out selling life insurance.

We'd sold the wig store and were thinking about selling the house. It was hard to come home every day and not find Uhmmah cooking junyuk in the kitchen. Whenever I looked over at the piano I could still hear her telling me to practice my scales.

I'd slipped and fallen on the floor at work the night before, and when my friend Davison had reached down to help me up, I'd shoved his hand away.

"Hey, *excuse me,*" he'd said, stepping back with his arms raised. My bare hands sliding all over the slick, greasy floor, I'd stood up, straightened my visor, and gone back to serving popcorn and soda. We didn't speak to each other the rest of the night, though by the time we'd locked up and I was waiting outside for Ahpbah to come pick me up, I was feeling pretty sorry about being such a jerk, which had made me madder than I already was. That I didn't know what I was mad about in the first place infuriated me further. My hands had been clenched white as I'd watched Davison drive away in his Volvo. It had been a stupid accident — had happened before, in fact — but right then I'd wanted so much to blame someone. I'd wanted there to be a *cause* for what had happened. But there wasn't. Which was exactly what I had a hard time accepting about Uhmmah.

When I woke up in the morning I didn't feel any better. I decided I was going to call in sick, then zoned out on some soap operas. After *General Hospital* ended in tears, I called up Sue to ask her if she wanted to go to Galveston. We hadn't spoken since the funeral.

"Galveston," she said. "How're you going to get there?"

"Cab," I said. "I've got one on the way. I can swing by and pick you up."

"You got a job now?"

"Yeah, I'm working down at the Cineplex."

"Does that mean you can get me in for free?"

"Depends."

"On what?"

"On if you're coming or not."

The waves crashed against the beach and sighed back into the ocean. Sue and I were sitting on a bench along the sea wall, our hands jammed into our coat pockets. I was wearing a green knit cap topped by a white yarn pom-pom. It said JETS on the front. Sue had pulled it out of her backpack once we'd gotten to the beach.

The wind whipped past my ears. The brown-gray of the water was only slightly darker than the color of the sky. It was the middle of October and unusually chilly. I could see tiny, faraway oil rigs blinking faintly.

I thought I heard something and turned to find Sue looking at me. Past her I could see our cab driver eating pistachios as he leaned against the side of the car. He was costing me a week's worth of buttering popcorn. Sue's hair, which had grown out and was naturally curly, waved across her face. "Did you say something?"

"What?"

"Huh?"

"Did you hear me?"

"No. What'd you say?"

"I asked you what the first thing you remembered about her was."

"Who?"

"Your mom, Jin-Han."

"Oh." I looked back out at the ocean and slouched even more. All I could think about was the sound of the waves.

"Jin-Han?"

The first thing I remembered about Uhmmah? I was annoyed by the question. I didn't want to think about it, and how it made me feel. I closed my eyes and leaned my head back on the bench. A flurry of images, sounds, and smells washed over me. A hopeful ice-cream truck drove past with its endless song. Seagulls squawked like they were supposed to.

Suddenly I opened my eyes and I was there all over again, two years old, losing my hat. . . .

John Son:
My Personal Journey

In 1965, each of my parents left Korea for Germany in search of a better life and work prospects. My father worked as a miner and part-time bandleader; my mother worked as a nurse. A couple of years later, they met and soon got married. After I was born, they decided to head for America. Though my family didn't arrive directly from Korea, their reasons for immigrating to America were the same: to have greater opportunities for themselves, their children, their children's children, and so on. But as a kid, I couldn't think that far ahead, and when Uhmmah and Ahpbah told me that was why I had to study so hard and set my goals so high, it drove me crazy. What did that have to do with being a kid?

By the time we landed in Chicago in 1971, changes to the United States immigration laws had made it easier, especially for skilled workers like nurses and engineers, to immigrate into the country. An explosion in the Asian immigrant population followed, and among the first wave of Korean immigrants, wig stores were one of the most popular ways of setting up shop. It was a natural connection, since most wigs were manufactured in Korea.

But it wasn't until I started going to school that I realized that owning a wig store *wasn't* that common. And that maybe it was just plain weird. And, like most kids, I didn't like having the word "weird" associated with my name, which was already weird enough: Hyun-Suck Son. (Every year I had to pronounce it correctly for a new teacher.) It made me resentful of my parents.

But we'd come to this country to stay, and through hard work and perseverance, my parents made a success of their lives in a place where they could never quite get a handle on the language. (If today the roles were to be reversed, and I tried to get a business off the ground in Korea, I don't know how successful I'd be.) After struggling in Chicago for a few years, and then in Memphis, the wig store took off in Houston. Soon we stopped living in cramped apartment complexes and moved into a brand-new house. Like Jin-Han's family, we bought a piano and I took lessons and went to private school. I got an Atari game system when it came out, and then later, an Apple IIe personal computer.

When I was growing up in Houston, there weren't a lot of Asian kids around. I was usually the only Asian kid in my class. In fact, Asians were called Orientals before it became politically correct to say Asian. But whatever the "right" term was, it didn't change the way I felt, or who I was. As the years went by, my classmates got used to having a Korean boy grow up in their midst. After all, I talked the same, studied the same subjects, watched the same sitcoms, listened to the same music, and, like my Mexican classmates, I spoke another language at home, though not necessarily well. For dinner we almost always had Korean food, but I also loved, and still do, a good burger, chicken-fried steak, and barbecue ribs. Between bulgogi and corn dogs is where I grew up, and that's the experience I've tried to get across in *Finding My Hat*.

Like Jin-Han's uhmmah, my uhmmah also passed away from stomach cancer. But I was much older than Jin-Han when it happened, and I'm thankful for the time I had with Uhmmah while she was here.

While I was writing *Finding My Hat*, I finally traveled to Korea for the first time. I met dozens of relatives I didn't even know I had. I found out I was the oldest of my cousins, and that if I'd grown up there, I would've had to shoulder the responsibility of representing my generation in our extended family. But since I wasn't there, the next oldest male cousin had to fill my shoes. He laughingly said that I owed him for all the things he'd had to do in my place, but still took time off from work to show me the country he loved — one he wouldn't trade for any other.

And I could see why. Though smaller than the state of Texas, Korea is a beautiful, scenic, mountainous peninsula with more than a thousand years of history and rich tradition. Divided into North and South Korea after World War II, the South Korea I visited wasn't very different from any of the places in which I grew up in America. There are malls, cell phones, and big-screen TVs showing Korean music videos. The thing that seemed most different to me, and that finally I grew tired of, was the lack of diversity. Nearly everyone was Korean. And living as I now do in New York City, I missed seeing people of all colors, shapes, and sizes. I missed hearing the pleasing sounds of a dozen different languages being spoken along the length of one block, reminding me that I'm only one story among countless others.

In the end, I left Korea feeling glad that I'd visited it — that I'd met all my relatives and saw where and how they lived. Some of them reminded me of Ahpbah, some of them Uhmmah, some of them my sister, and some of them me. It made me see where I had come from, and discover the rich culture and long history that I realized was a part of me — in my blood — and always would be. At the same time, I couldn't wait to get back to America, my home.

Glossary

ahjushi — mister
ahpbah — father
ahruhsuh — understand
Aigoo — Oh my; What?!;
    That's crazy!
bahnchahn — side dishes
bbahli — hurry
bibimbap — rice casserole
bohrheecha — barley tea
bulgogi — barbecued beef
Chahmnah — My goodness
dong-sehng — younger sibling
eemoh — aunt on uhmmah's side
gohmoh — aunt on ahpbah's side
hahlmuhnee — grandmother
hahrahbuhjee — grandfather
hanbok — dress
Hangook — Korea
Hangul — the Korean language
jahguhn ahpbah — uncle on
    ahpbah's side, his younger
    brother
junyuk — dinner
kahlbi — marinated short ribs
kimbap — rice rolled in dried
    seaweed with bulgogi
    (sometimes Spam when
    Uhmmah didn't have time!),
    spinach, cucumber, and
    pickled radish

kimchi — spicy, pickled cabbage
khochu — hot pepper
khochujang — hot pepper paste
khori komtang — oxtail soup
kuhn ahpbahs — uncle on
    ahpbah's side, his older
    brother
mandu — dumpling
mehkjoo — beer
Mi Gook — America
Mohllah — I don't know.
Moh rah gooh — What did you
    say?
Nehmseh chohtah — It smells
    great.
ohpbah — brother
Ominah — Watch out; Ohmygod;
    Holy #?@!
sahmcheun — uncle on
    uhmmah's side
uhmmah — mother
yoboh — spouse

Acknowledgments

This book wouldn't have happened if my editor, Amy Griffin, hadn't talked me into writing it. Without her confidence in my story, and her stellar and unerring editorial eye, I wouldn't have had the life-filling experience that *Finding My Hat* turned out to be. And I will always be grateful.

Thanks to my awesome sister, Agnes, who knows a lot more about being Korean-American than me. And of course Ahpbah, for filling in details and telling me stories about his life. And for helping me become who I am.

Also thanks to Lauren Monchik for her daily support, enthusiasm, and encouragement, as well as the rest of my friends who've been there throughout the writing of the book. And special mention to Sung Rno and Terri Huh for their assistance in the spelling of Korean words.

And finally the wonderful crew at Scholastic: Jean Feiwel, Elizabeth Parisi, Kerrie Baldwin, and Lisa Sandell.

Find Yourself in
FIRST PERSON FICTION

A new series about coming to America

Behind the Mountains
Edwidge Danticat

Celiane and her family escape from politically unstable and impoverished Haiti only to find a new set of challenges in the concrete jungle of New York.

Flight to Freedom
Ana Veciana-Suarez

Yara's moving account tells her family's story of exile from Cuba and adjustment to life in a less traditional country.

Look for news about the First Person Student Writing Contest on the scholastic.com Kids site.